Ever Together

by

Margie L. Miller

This is a work of fiction. Names, characters, places, and incidents are either the product of the author's imagination or are used fictitiously, and any resemblance to actual persons living or dead, business establishments, events, or locales, is entirely coincidental.

Ever Together

Cover Art by *Kim Mendoza*

The Wild Rose Press
PO Box 708
Adams Basin, NY 14410-0708
Visit us at www.thewildrosepress.com

Publishing History
First Sweetheart Rose Edition, 2012
Print ISBN 978-1-62830-314-8
Digital ISBN 978-1-61217-136-4

Published in the United States of America

"Why did you lie to me?" she asked with a wobbly voice. "Why didn't you tell me the truth?"

She was trying not to cry, and Caleb felt completely helpless. He could handle anger. If she was yelling at him right now, he'd be fine. But her misery was out of his depth and he felt like he was drowning.

He could tell her that he technically never lied. But he knew he hadn't been completely forthcoming either. That was really what she was asking. She felt deceived.

"I was only supposed to be here for one night," he started softly. "I didn't know..." he paused, searching for the right words but his mind was blank. "I just didn't know," he repeated.

He didn't know that in such a short time, she'd completely bewitch him, and he didn't know how on earth he was going to reconcile the huge gap between his notoriety and the life she'd built for herself here. So he had closed his eyes and pretended he could be with her, that everything was normal—that *he* was normal.

Sliding downward until he was on the floor, he bent his knees upward and folded his arms over his stomach. He closed his eyes and leaned his head against the wall. "You were so incredible." He paused, trying to find the right words. "And you saw *me*, and I wanted you to keep seeing *me*." He opened his eyes again, staring at her hair and willing her to look at him. "When I realized I couldn't leave you, I knew I'd have to tell you the truth, but I didn't know how."

"'I have to have five bodyguards follow me around' would have been a good start," she told him acidly, finally raising her eyes to glare at him.

"I didn't want to ruin the day," he said weakly, and she scoffed. "Look, I'm sorry," he pleaded. "More sorry than you will ever know."

Dedication

Thank you to my cheerleaders:
Wanda, Gina and Chris.
Thank you, Arlisa,
for helping to make a scene sigh-worthy.
Thank you, Kari,
for being critical when I needed you to be.
And mostly, thank you to my husband,
for being so understanding of my passions.

Chapter One

Katy heard the jingle of the bells attached to the front glass door and hastily threw her book under the counter, swallowing her irritation. The hero was only one village away from reuniting with his wife, and she just *knew* the moment they found each other would be gut-wrenching and amazing. The fact that she had to pull herself from the story to deal with the only late night customer she'd had in a week only fueled her resentment. Whoever this midnight traveler was, their timing sucked.

Her eyes lifted to the man standing between a rack of chips and a display of newspapers, and her heart flipped over before plummeting to her knees. The stranger looked ominous. His wavy, unnaturally black hair was short in the back, but tapered until the front bangs were long enough to tickle his chin on either side of his face. His dark eyes were bloodshot and scraggy stubble covered his jaw.

According to the tape markings on the door, he stood about six foot five, and he was wearing loose fitting black jeans draped with a silver chain that extended from a front belt loop to circle around to his back. On his left wrist was a wide black leather band and his blue shirt had a massive skull on the front.

His red-rimmed eyes surveyed the area. She was sure he was casing the store, the dollar amount he could score, and the booze on hand. If he decided to rob her, he'd only get forty dollars, and five of that was from her own purse. Quietly, she shuffled her position behind the register and gripped the handle of the wooden bat that had leaned against the counter for months.

Suddenly, she didn't feel like laughing at her boss anymore. "This is Hoboken-No-Where, Steve. Everyone knows I don't have any cash in here at night. What do I need protection from?"

She'd apologize to him in the morning and bake him his favorite chocolate chip cookies if she lived through this. Was the stranger high?

The man's dark eyes finally rested on her and he shuffled further into the convenience store, causing her to tense and grip the bat tighter in her right fist as morbid scenarios circled ruthlessly through her mind.

"Hello," she managed. Her voice sounded strained in her own ears, and she felt like her heart was going to thud right out of her chest. Fight or flight. *Fight or flight.*

"Excuse me," he said, his voice low and gravelly but oddly polite. "Are you Katy?"

****

Caleb was beyond tired. His day had started twenty three hours ago, at one in the morning, and proceeded through sixteen hours of work before this last seven hour marathon drive through the backwoods of nowhere. The road trip had been his own fault; he'd acted on impulse and desperation. But he couldn't go another mile, though he was really wishing he could.

The mere fact that he was considering following the hotel manager's advice spoke volumes about his state of mind. For a full ten minutes, he'd sat outside the small store, watching the clerk through the glass door as she not-so-subtly read her book.

She'd been enthralled, eyes widening with emotion, back stiffening as she turned the page. She was in her early twenties, a little on the plain side, and worked in a lousy job—all the markers of the obsessed fans who stalked his every move.

His gut clenched and he squeezed his eyes tightly for a moment as he calmed his breathing. It was just one woman. Not a mob. Who cared if she recognized him? Alone, she couldn't do any damage.

Her copper colored hair fell into her eyes, and she brushed it back absently, tucking it behind her ear. Suddenly, his earlier impulse for freedom was squashed and Caleb desperately missed the comfort of the presence of his security detail.

Taking another deep breath, he pushed on the glass door and stepped into the brightly lit store. Instantly, the young woman jumped and threw her book under the counter. He watched through his peripheral vision as she looked up at him, and he inwardly cringed inside when she stiffened, her eyes wide.

Any second now, the screaming would start.

He waited a few moments, pretending to survey the store's contents before turning to the clerk. No screaming yet. Her breaths were coming in small gasps and he saw that she reached next to her behind the counter, grabbing some unseen object.

"Hello," she greeted calmly, the composure in her voice at odds with her body language. Was she working up the nerve to ask for an autograph?

"Excuse me," he said with a voice roughened by fatigue, desperate to get this over with. "Are you Katy?"

If it were possible, her body went on higher alert and her green eyes narrowed. "Who's asking?" she demanded suspiciously.

Who's asking? Relief flooded through him, and he was almost giddy with joy. Either his costume was beyond excellent, or he'd finally come across a woman who didn't know who he was. He wanted to gather her into his arms, hug her tightly and say "thank you."

He knew he was paranoid. To an outsider, he would appear the pinnacle of arrogant and self-absorbed. But three years of being mobbed every single time he stepped outside his own apartment had ruthlessly taught him not to underestimate the tenacity of the paparazzi and the female mind. He never once left his home or job site without a camera flash going off in his face and someone screaming "Derrick! I love you!"

Two years ago in Texas there'd almost been a riot outside the restaurant where he was eating lunch. Nearly eight hundred women and teenagers had crushed the parking lot, and it had taken seven burly men acting as human shields to get him through the crowd unmolested.

In the beginning, he assured himself that this kind of attention was fleeting. The next heartthrob would invariably make a more popular movie and he'd be saved all the scrutiny. He'd be able to blow his nose without a telescopic lens immortalizing the moment over the internet, but three years later he was still waiting. He was tired of it. He had never wanted it in the first place. All he wanted was to act.

But the clerk was staring at him, waiting for him to pull his mind back to the present and answer her.

"The manager of the hotel said that Katy runs a bed-and-breakfast, and that I could find her working here." Somehow, the one motel in this backwater no-place was completely filled.

That news didn't surprise the clerk, though. She relaxed, smiling at him and nodded knowingly. "Ah, yes, the Johnson's family reunion. Four generations ago, the mom and pop had twelve children, who each had over seven, who each had... well... enough anyways." She laughed, and put whatever she'd been grasping away and leaned against the counter next to her register.

Her elbows rested on top of the glass displaying the lottery tickets, and she clasped her hands together, twining her fingers and leaning heavily forward, closer to him. She was at ease now, and she looked quite comfortable in her flannel shirt and blue jeans. Her copper hair wisped around her face and she absently brushed it aside and behind her ear again.

"I'm afraid that Charlie made it sound grander than it is, really."

Caleb's heart sank. He didn't think he could drive the twenty miles to the next town on the map. "I'm not looking for anything fancy."

"Well, it's not a bed and breakfast in the strictest sense of the term." Her mouth lifted on one corner, her eye scrunching downward to meet it in consternation. "I've got a really big house with lots of spare rooms. You're welcome to one, if you want. You'll have to make your own bed, and I can get someone to make you a sandwich tonight, but you'll have to make your own breakfast," she warned. "You can eat anything at all in the kitchen that you want, with the exception of the cottage cheese. Jerry's on another diet."

Great. The thought of crashing in someone's spare room was unpleasant, and definitely out of his comfort zone, but he didn't have a choice. He could either accept this woman's hospitality, or he could sleep in his car. Before he could respond, she was already on the phone, dialing, and then listening intently.

"Teddy? Hi, it's me. Hey, I'm going to send someone over in a minute. His name is—" she paused, looking up at him expectantly.

"Caleb Smith," he told her, using his real name instead of his stage name. The longer he could stay under the radar, the better.

"Caleb," she spoke into the phone. "He's got

5

black hair and a blue shirt with a skull." She paused and then smiled. "Charlie sent him over to me." Another pause. "All right, all right. Give him the room next to Kyle. No, on the other side, near Jerry." Her smile grew wider. "Great, Teddy, you're the best. Show him where everything is, all right? Thank you!"

She hung up and turned her crinkly eyes and wide smile on him, her face completely transformed by her happiness. "You're all set. Teddy will be waiting on the porch for you."

"Uh, thank you. How much do I owe you?" he asked, wanting to pay her now so that he could just leave in the morning.

"Nothing," she answered. "If you eat anything, just put enough money to cover the cost of your food in the cookie jar on the fridge."

When Caleb felt his eyebrow rise in shock she smiled wider obviously accustomed to the reaction. "Honestly. It's all right. I wouldn't dream of accepting payment. You're crashing on an unused bed for a few hours. It's not a big deal."

"Thank you," he said, deciding to just leave a generous tip in the cookie jar. "Um... how do I get there?"

She laughed. "Oh yeah, you'll need directions won't you? It's two blocks that way," she informed him, pointing in the general direction she meant. "You can't miss it. It's the biggest house on the street, and there's a sign out front that says Gilfrey's on it."

He smiled his thanks and headed out to his car again, hoping he'd be able to find this house as easily as she claimed he could.

Chapter Two

Finding the house was no problem. It was, as promised, the largest building on the street. There were no lamps in the neighborhood, leaving the night amazingly dark, but a single yellow bulb shone on a wooden sign with the name "Gilfrey's" scripted across it in gold lettering.

Caleb pulled into the large circular driveway and followed the beacon of the lone porch light. A man stood on the porch, dressed in dark sweatpants and a yellow T-shirt. Parking behind a battered truck, Caleb grabbed his overnight bag from the passenger's seat and slung it over his shoulder as he cautiously stepped out of his car.

"Hello," he greeted the man on the porch. "I'm Caleb. Katy sent me here."

"Hey," the man said wearily. "I'm Ted. I'm supposed to show you around."

He held out a hand, and Caleb stepped onto the porch to shake it. Ted was in his early thirties, with blond hair that looked as though it spent the whole day under a hat of some kind, edges poofing out on the sides. Was he Katy's husband?

Caleb was too tired to take in his surroundings, the grogginess making his head fuzzy, and let the rambling of his host wash over him as he followed him into the house.

"We're pretty informal around here," his guide began. "Jerry made up a bed for you, and there's a sandwich on your nightstand."

They traveled through a dimly lit room with

couches and a fireplace, and headed for a stairwell.

"You'll have to make your own breakfast," Ted continued. "Just stay away from the cottage cheese, if you don't want to incur Jerry's wrath." His tone implied death and doom should that occur.

But Caleb wouldn't be here that long. After a few hours of sleep he'd be on the road again, probably headed back to the latest apartment his manager had rented for him. The thought depressed him.

Climbing the stairs at a leisurely pace, his guide kept up his monologue. "We have some informal rules here. If your door is closed, no one will bug you. If you leave it open, you are fair game. Be warned. Elizabeth likes to visit. If you like your music loud, use headphones. Katy sleeps until noon, so don't make any noise until she comes down on her own. It's hard to wake her, she's on the third floor and she sleeps like the dead. But we had an idiot here one time who—" Ted paused, stopping himself. "Well, never mind. Use common courtesy and you'll be fine."

He tossed a quick assessing glance over his shoulder. "There's three bathrooms in the house. One is in Katy's room in the attic. The closest is at the end of the hall, but the women have pretty much taken over that one. It's got the bathtub," he explained. "The other one is safer. Kyle and I generally use the one under the stairs, unless it's the middle of the night. The womenfolk are asleep now, so you'll be fine."

Now walking down a long wide hallway, they passed doors on either side until they reached the end. Caleb vaguely noted that the place was huge, but was too tired to keep count of the rooms.

"Here you go," Ted said, opening the last door and stepping out of the way. "If you need anything, I'm three doors down on the opposite side of you.

Just knock."

"Thanks," Caleb mumbled, stepping into the room and looking around him.

Ted closed the door, and he was alone.

The room was small, but the bed was already made, and the promised sandwich rested on a plate on the nightstand with a glass of water. Two steps in, and he was at the bed. There was room for a single chair and a small dresser. A large window on the opposite wall was covered with buttercup yellow curtains, which somehow seemed to match the purple rag throw-rug he was standing on. At the end of the bed was a handmade quilt, a hodgepodge of colors, the design intricate.

That was the extent of observation that Caleb could muster at the moment. Throwing his bag on the chair, he wolfed down the roast beef sandwich before quietly sneaking down the hall to use the facilities. After returning to his small room, he managed to rally enough energy to pull off the T-shirt and jeans he'd been wearing for three weeks before collapsing into bed. He was asleep before he noticed there wasn't a lock on the bedroom door.

****

Caleb woke to the sound of childish squealing and laughter emanating from outside. He groaned and rolled over, pulling a pillow over his face to block out the sunlight that streamed through the large window. It was no good, though. He wouldn't be able to fall back asleep.

Indulging in self-denial, he refused to move and simply lay in the full sized bed, keeping his body relaxed and thinking about his arrival at this strange place.

The children outside laughed again and Caleb eventually roused himself to sit up. A digital clock on the nightstand caught his eye, and he was astonished that it said one p.m. He had slept for thirteen hours straight. Livy was going to skin him alive.

Sighing, he reached over to his bag, plopped it onto the quilt next to him and pulled out his cell phone. He had forty three voicemails and a hundred and seven text messages. Ignoring them all, he pushed the speed dial button and waited briefly. Livy answered halfway through the first ring.

"Where on earth are you?" she asked angrily as a greeting.

He knew his family would have already learned about his disappearance. He normally tried to give them a warning about news items before they hit the internet. Spotting a rock on the windowsill, he grasped it in his hands and began to idly twirl it in his fingers as he answered. "Look, I'm sorry—"

"Don't 'sorry' me, what were you thinking? Where have you been? Are you all right? Mom is worried sick! Your ex-girlfriend called—"

"I'm fine." Some hurts were better left buried in the past. "Tell Mom I needed to get away for a while."

Livy's voice softened. "Do you need to come home? We'd love to see you. You don't start filming again for a few weeks, right? Come home and let Mom cook for you."

He wished he could. He missed his little sister and his parents. "I'll try to come for a visit soon," he promised. His family stoically endured the media coverage whenever he went there, but it was an ordeal he tried to minimize. The last time, his father had punched a photographer in the nose. "Do me a favor and call Abigail. Tell her that I'm fine, and I'll contact her before the Chicago interviews, all right?"

"Sure, no problem," his sister assured him. "She's been calling here every thirty minutes anyway. Your manger is tenacious, isn't she?"

"That's why I hired her," he said with a smile.

Abigail was very good at her job, arranging his life and protecting him from all the stalkers while keeping him accessible to the non-crazy fans. In two and a half years of working together she'd never once made a pass at him.

He absently placed the rock on the nightstand next to the clock, realizing that there were two more stones already there.

"Oh hey, Caleb?" Livy asked, her voice sounding embarrassed. "Can I borrow thirty bucks until next Friday when I get paid? There's a dance this weekend, and there's this really great dress on sale at Milton's—"

He laughed. "No problem, Liv. Go ahead and use the card. You don't have to ask, and you don't have to pay it back."

He knew it was pointless to say so. She always asked before using the debit card he'd given her. And despite his protestations, she always paid him back when she earned enough money from her summer job.

"Thanks, Caleb. You're my hero."

He smiled ruefully. He was more than happy to buy her a dress. And shoes to go with it, if she wanted. But his family consistently turned down his help. His parents had flatly refused when he tried to pay off their mortgage and the loan on their vehicles. So here he was, earning seven digits with every movie he made, with nothing to spend it on.

"Tell Mom I love her, and I'll call back later."

"All right. Be safe."

"You to. Love you."

"Love ya more," she answered with a smile in her voice before hanging up.

He missed her again already. She was eight years his junior, and only sixteen, but she was his best friend right now. Maybe he could make it home. The photographers had lost his trail, maybe he could make it there without being noticed.

He dismissed the thought as soon as it entered his mind. He hadn't cleared a single airport in over three years without his picture being taken and a TSA agent asking for an autograph for their daughter. Those people were innocent enough, but word always got out, and piranhas soon followed. There was no way.

Sighing, he got up out of bed and dressed in his own clothes, glad to be rid of the costume at last. Pulling on his favorite blue jeans and white T-shirt, he ran his fingers through his hair before stuffing on his sneakers. The black mop flopped over his eyes and he grimaced. It was naturally wavy when it grew out, but he rarely ever let it get to this length, preferring it short. He reminded himself that soon, he'd be shaving his head for the next role, so both the length and unnatural color would be gone.

He pulled a wad of cash from his wallet without counting it and stuffed it in the front pocket of his jeans before packing all his belongings into his bag and slinging it over his shoulder.

Grabbing the plate and glass from the nightstand, he headed out his door, intent on finding the cookie jar and making a silent escape. The house was quiet, and every door in the hallway stood open. No one was around, but the sight of his surroundings made him pause. He'd been too tired during his initial trip through the corridor to notice, but it was decorated in countless handprints.

Every size, every color imaginable covered the surface. Small hands were at the bottom of the wall, growing larger as they ascended. Every palm had a date printed neatly across it in black permanent marker. The oldest one he could see was forty five years old. Near the ceiling, green leafy vines crisscrossed down the hallway, almost as though pointing the way to the exit.

The painted foliage continued down the stairwell, intermingling with random pictures. There was a fairy and a frog, an umbrella, grapes, a clown. There didn't seem to be any rhyme or reason to the arrangements.

At the bottom of the stairs, he was in the living area. It was larger than he'd imagined the previous night. He had no idea how he'd missed the mural of a beach that covered one entire wall. The couches were leather, overstuffed, and brown. They faced the fireplace, positioned in a semi-circle. In another corner of the large room was another set of smaller sofas, circled around a small television set.

On the wall behind the television was another mural of a winter landscape. It was partially finished, and he could make out the faint penciled outlines of deer, more trees, and a cabin.

He liked it. There was absolutely nothing pretentious about this place. It was as though someone had gotten into the mood to paint and was given free rein to color at will. It reminded him of the time when he was seven and had colored on the dining room wall with colored markers, and his mom had framed it.

The frame and the picture were still there, as a matter of fact.

His eyes found a doorway under the stairs, and he quickly made use of the "man bathroom" before trekking out to locate the cookie jar. He wasn't in quite as much of a hurry now. The more he saw of this house, the more he liked it. As soon as he paid his bill, he had no reason to stay.

Wandering, he followed the sound of voices and ended up walking into a massive kitchen, lighted with huge windows. Beyond the windows was a view of the squealing and laughing children as they ran and tumbled and played on an enormous tree house and wooden jungle gym, complete with swings, slides, turrets, rope ladders, and other various items he couldn't identify.

Katy stood at a large stove in pink plaid, flannel pajama pants, and a lime green cotton T-shirt. On her feet were two pink fuzzy bunnies, with long pointy ears reaching toward her shins. Their brownish-black eyes stared up at him beseechingly, and their little mouths were pulled up into innocent smiles.

He couldn't help but do the same.

Her copper colored hair was pulled back into a ponytail that was losing its fight against gravity. Wisps had escaped and trailed over her face and down her neck, forcing his eyes to follow the trail. He realized he must have been very tired the previous evening; she was anything but plain. One hand was enshrouded with a massive green mitten; the other wielded a spatula that she was waving in the air toward a woman sitting at the table.

The other woman was older, her hair white, with her bangs pulled back neatly into barrettes. Her face was weathered and slightly wrinkly. She was wearing an orange, paint-splattered smock and she was smiling widely.

He shuffled his feet and both sets of eyes turned to him.

There was a slight pause for a second. Someone gasped. But it was only a moment; he may have imagined it, because his hostess was now waving the spatula in his direction.

"Oh! Good! You're up!" Katy announced, smiling at him. "I made too much breakfast. Please tell me you're hungry, because this'll just go to waste if you don't help us eat it."

Before he could answer and refuse her generosity, she had already dropped the spatula on the counter and was retrieving another plate from a cupboard, setting a place for him. "Elizabeth, this is

Caleb. Caleb, Elizabeth. He joined us last night. Charlie's place was filled up with the Johnsons." She waved for him to sit at the table.

Elizabeth chuckled. "Hello, Caleb, nice to meet you."

"Likewise," he said as he followed Katy's directive to the seat, wondering why he didn't feel awkward or uncomfortable. He lowered himself into the wooden frame, placing the used plate and glass on the table and dropping his bag under his chair. "I was admiring your work in the other room. You are very good."

Elizabeth ducked her head and blushed lightly. "Oh, I have fun. It keeps me busy."

Katy beamed at him, and he realized that he'd inadvertently won brownie points by complimenting the artist.

"So you're on a trip," the older woman changed the subject. "How fun! I used to travel a lot. Where are you headed, if I may ask?"

He looked the woman in the eyes for a second, and could only see companionable curiosity. She was warm and inviting. As Ted had said the previous night, she liked to visit. "I don't know," he said. "I haven't made up my mind yet."

****

Oh good. No plans. Katy could see Elizabeth immediately start making some for him, knowing the magic of Tolleson. No one ever left after only one night. "Are you on vacation?" she asked, trying to formulate excursions that might interest him.

"Sorta," he said, shrugging. "I'm between jobs right now."

Katy knew her older friend well enough she could almost hear the woman's thoughts as though spoken aloud. "Oh dear, he was out of work," flitted across her eyes, then "That would explain his grungy outfit and bad haircut."

15

Katy's heart went out to Caleb, knowing what it was like to struggle for money. But she had a home, friends, and family. She had roots, and money didn't matter when you had all that. She had plenty to share, and what was hers could be his. Jerry would no doubt lecture her about bringing home yet another "vagrant" as she called them. She always did.

The pity she was feeling must have been transparent on her face, because Caleb smiled.

"My next gig doesn't start for a couple of months, and I'm taking time off to recuperate."

Still watching this man interact with her roommate, Katy smiled as Elizabeth's hands fluttered to her chest, over her heart.

"Are you a musician?" her friend asked. "How exciting."

"No," he said, his eyes darting to Katy, and then back to the older woman warily. "I'm an actor." He waited, holding his breath to see their reaction.

He would receive no condemnation from either of them. As Elizabeth had once said, if a person was happy scraping by with their creative endeavors, she applauded them. "How wonderful!" her friend exclaimed. "Are you any good?"

He panicked. The twitch in his eyes was very subtle, but his breathing shifted and he began to tap his leg with his fingers. He didn't want to talk about this for some reason, but it was apparent Elizabeth was not going to see his discomfort and drop the conversation anytime soon.

"Caleb, do you like pancakes?" Katy asked, interrupting the interrogation in an effort to relieve some of his anxiety. One thing she'd learned long ago: men relaxed better on a full stomach.

He smiled at her gratefully. "Yes, I do." Several were plopped onto his plate, and he began to butter them.

"How about scrambled eggs?"

"I like scrambled eggs," he answered, and a spoonful of yellow mash was glopped onto plate next to the pancakes.

"Bacon and sausage?" She didn't wait for his answer before piling several pieces of bacon and a couple slices of sausage onto his dish.

She rummaged in the fridge, pulled out cream cheese and bagels, then finished off by placing a fruit bowl in the center of the banquet. That ought to be enough to feed a man who might not have eaten regularly for a while.

She dropped into the seat across from him, and began loading up her plate. In an attempt to make him feel less shy, and let him know that he could eat as much as he wanted, she piled her plate high. The pancakes and eggs and sausages rivaled Caleb's in their quantity, plus she scooped on a generous spoonful of watermelon.

It was in his best interests. The man across from her had the look of someone who should weigh a few more pounds than he currently did. He needed to stick around for a little while. Long enough to get some meat on his bones and recuperate from sleeping in his car.

Elizabeth sighed beside them, probably grossed out with her landlady's mountain of food.

"Well, if you don't know where you're going," Katy began, as if there hadn't been any interruption in the conversation, "it doesn't matter where you go or where you end up, does it?" She stuffed her mouth with scrambled eggs and chewed thoughtfully, piercing Caleb with her direct stare.

He met her gaze, and she felt her stomach flip over as his eyes held hers in thrall. He only shrugged, ignoring his food. "I guess not," he admitted.

"Then why don't you stay here for a few days?"

she asked him, popping a piece of watermelon through her teeth. "The annual summer bash is coming up soon. It's a lot of fun."

She stopped talking to chew, reminding herself not to start speaking again until all the food was cleared out of her mouth. Then, finally finding the strength to look away from him, she concentrated on her plate.

He cleared his throat and wouldn't raise his eyes again. "I don't know," he said, shrugging. "The hotel is full and—"

"Oh, that's no problem," Katy said. "It's not like anyone else was using your room." She smiled at him around her pancakes. Remembering her manners, she took a moment to chew and swallow before taking a swig of orange juice and continuing. "Don't think I'm trying to trap you here or anything, but you looked really bad last night." Aw crud. Embarrassment began to creep its way through as she realized she just insulted the man.

But a friend told the truth no matter how awful, and last night, he looked like a man on the brink of a breakdown. He *still* looked like he was teetering on the edge, despite his marathon nap. And he looked lonely. She was a sucker for lonely.

"You could get decent rest here. It's generally quiet—" a child shrieked outside, which she chose to ignore, "—and we'd leave you alone if you want. Or I'm sure Elizabeth would be willing to act as tour guide and show you all the wonderful sights."

He looked at them both warily, undecided. What did he see?

"I'm not sure," he admitted.

He probably thought they were all crazy.

"Please? The more the merrier. Come and go as you please. Stay as long or as short as you want. But if you don't have anywhere else to go, you are welcome here."

Why was she pushing so hard? She was practically begging.

That awful hair of his flopped down into his face when he lowered his eyes to his food. She knew instinctively that he didn't trust her, and even though he was a stranger, that made her sad. If he stayed, wonderful. If not, she would mourn the loss of her almost-friend later.

It was time to drop the subject. "So what do you do in your free time?" He looked momentarily confused by her abrupt shift, but he shook his head with a small smile as if to clear his mind, and speared a piece of sausage with his fork. "Um... I haven't had much free time lately. I'm usually working. But I love to read," he said, pausing momentarily and appearing to search his memory. "I visit my family when I can," he said with a far-away look in his eyes.

Then he smiled and her heart puddled somewhere in the region of her stomach. Her hands began to shake and she had to remind herself to breathe. The sensation was not altogether unpleasant, and she finally admitted to herself that she also had more selfish reasons for wanting him to stay.

He made her feel good, simply by being there. Whenever he smiled, or cast those dark brown eyes on her, she felt giddy. No one could blame a girl for wanting that around. It was like being on a caffeine rush, without having to actually drink the six-pack of Jolt. She'd done it once, on a bet, and the sensation was surprisingly similar.

Ever since Katy saw Caleb standing in her kitchen doorway looking lonely and tired, she didn't want to let him go. He needed them. Something inside her told her that he would fit into their hodgepodge family, and she wanted the opportunity to help him.

Loud shouting from outside interrupted her musings and Brandy Ellison's hurried footsteps and panicked voice shouted through the glass. "Miss Simms! Miss Simms! Come quick! Trudy fell down and got hurt!"

All thoughts about Caleb and his plight and how he made her feel evaporated, instantly replaced with a mental review of basic first aid as she jumped from her seat. Hurrying to the kitchen door and grabbing the well-used kit from the counter without breaking stride, Katy made the familiar charge to the playground, grateful that Elizabeth would make any phone calls necessary.

Chapter Three

Caleb sat on a couch near the TV, staring out the window at the night sky and sipping idly at a can of cream soda while he remembered his amazing day. He laughed to himself, picturing Katy in her flannel pajama pants and bunny slippers, administering first aid to the crying six-year-old. She had cleaned up the bloody mouth with a washcloth, administered a Spiderman bandage and waited patiently with the little girl until a young mother had arrived to take her child to the urgent care center for x-rays.

Katy didn't even mind that her shirt had been stained with blood and tears. He was happy, though, that the bunnies had made it through the ordeal unscathed, with the exception of a little dust. He was fond of them.

Thanks to Elizabeth's love of chatting and the fact that he'd spent the whole day with her, he now had a grasp on this massive house, who these eclectic people were, and what their relationship was to each other. The glue, the connection, was Katy. Ted was not her husband. He was, in fact, her cousin, the son of her mother's sister, staying here until his house sold and he could move his wife and daughter with him. He'd been laid off from his job last year, and found work as a field hand at a local farm.

Kyle was a nineteen year old boy whose motorcycle had broken down outside of town. When he stopped by the Slurp-N-Go to spend his last dollar on a bag of chips for dinner, Katy took him home for a square meal. He was now working at the same farm as Ted and taking night courses at the community college thirty miles away in Westerbrook. He wanted to be an Aeronautical Engineer and was dating a local girl.

Elizabeth had been on vacation. She was canoeing down the river a short half mile out of town and stopped for a picnic lunch. Katy had been hiking past and stopped to chat. They shared lunch, and the older woman came back to the house to see Katy's garden. She never left.

Jerry was an enigma to Caleb, and he smiled to himself as he thought of her. She was a sophisticated, professional woman who worked as an accountant in Westerbrook, and she commuted every day back and forth to her job site. He took a swig of his soda and rested his elbows on his knees as he thought about meeting her earlier that evening, after the playground incident.

He'd been standing at a wall in the living room, a paint pallet in one hand and a brush in the other, receiving an art lesson from Elizabeth and listening to Kyle strum his guitar. Katy sat on the couch in her jeans and a flannel shirt reading a book when the front door blew open to reveal Jerry, the cottage cheese lover.

Everything about her was sleek and properly placed. Her chestnut colored hair was pulled into a bun, and no wisps dared to break free. Even after a full day, her dress was uncrumpled. Her make-up looked as though she'd just put it on.

Her heels were at least two inches tall, but she stood erect, firm and confident. The briefcase in her hand was made of expensive leather and the purse slung over her shoulder was a Tiffany's. He'd bet his next paycheck on it. He'd bought a couple as gifts for Livy, who had a weakness for the brand.

She looked like she belonged in a boardroom, in command of a multi-million-dollar corporation. It was intimidating, if he were thoroughly honest with himself.

Noting all of this took only the space of a single breath. His second thought was to wonder why she was on a diet. She wasn't thin, but her curves suited her. Her face was softer for the lack of severe angles, and despite her no-nonsense outfit, she seemed... he mentally paused for a moment, searching for the right word, and finally settled on "approachable."

She stepped into the house, smiling at Katy and pushing the door closed behind her with her high-heeled foot. Turning as the door clicked, she caught sight of Caleb for the first time.

All the color drained from her face, her foundation useless. Her expensive leather briefcase crashed to the floor and her jaw dropped open as a low gagging sound choked from the back of her throat.

Oh no, he thought to himself as his heart sunk to his knees. Everything would be over now, he was sure of it.

"You're..." Jerry began, "You're De—"

"Hello," he interrupted her with a smile. "My name is Caleb Smith." He spoke as he put down his pallet and brush and crossed the room to her, holding out his hand. Even if this woman had the power to send him home, he would still be polite.

Jerry raised an eyebrow doubtfully, but reached a shaking hand out to grasp his.

"Hello," she said, a little breathless. She caught the silent pleading in his eyes and continued, "...Mr. Smith."

He breathed in deeply and flashed his biggest smile, eternally grateful. Maybe she'd blackmail him later, but for now, he was going to take her at face value. "Please, just call me Caleb."

She nodded, mute for a second. It was embarrassing, really. For the millionth time, he wondered why women reacted that way. She was older than him, a professional, beautiful woman, obviously smart and successful. But because some photographers knew how to dress him properly and catch him in the right light, she was star-struck. Someday, he was going to belch at just the wrong moment. Then maybe he'd be human again.

"Can I ha—" she stopped herself, blushing, and shook her head. After a moment staring at him, she breathed in deeply, gathered her composure, firmly shook his hand and picked up her briefcase. Once again, she was the sophisticated woman, in charge of her life. "It's nice to meet you, Caleb. I hope you enjoy your stay with us."

She marched past him and up the stairs, disappearing at the landing.

"That was weird," Katy murmured from the couch, looking after Jerry with concern.

Before anyone could comment further, Ted stuck his head through the kitchen door. "Hamburgers are done!" he called.

Dinner later that night had reminded Caleb of summer family barbecues. A picnic table in the backyard had been set up buffet style, and everyone grabbed the baked beans, burgers, toppings and chips at their leisure, occasionally bumping into each other, or fighting over the mustard.

Jerry arrived a few minutes later in jeans and a T-shirt, her hair now in a simple braid and holding a giant plastic tub and a silver colored spoon. She eyed the table longingly, but stoically dug into her cottage cheese. She looked hungry. She looked like she was loathing the cottage cheese.

Caleb added an extra scooping of the fruit pieces leftover from lunch onto his plate and purposely sat next to the dieter, placing the plate slightly in her direction. "Thank you, Jerry," he said softly. The others were arguing over a baseball game played last weekend in town, and he knew they wouldn't be heard.

"I don't know what you're talking about," she denied, eyeing his plate.

He stabbed a piece of cantaloupe and dropped it into her container, watching it plop amongst the curds. "Yes, you do. Thank you."

She scooped the fruit into her spoon and quickly shoveled it into her mouth, as though eating it quickly would negate its presence.

"Normally, I don't mind subterfuge like this," she told him as he plopped a couple of grapes into her cheese. "But this is Katy." The two grapes disappeared into her mouth and her eyes closed, savoring the taste of the juice gushing over her tongue. She chewed slowly and then swallowed reluctantly. "I don't like lying to her. I won't lie to her."

He chose a piece of watermelon next, and watched it disappear. "I'm not lying to her," he assured. "My name *is* Caleb Smith: Caleb Derrick Smith, actually."

"And the 'Nelson'?" she asked, referring to the last name everyone knew him by.

"It's my mother's maiden name," he answered.

There was a moment of silence as he bit into a chip and Jerry ate the strawberry he'd given her.

"Why are you still here?" she asked softly.

Since she was already informed about the hotel problem, he knew what her real question was. He paused as he considered his answer, munching softly and covertly pushing more fruit into the still-full cottage cheese container. "I'm here because Katy asked me to stay," he answered at last, wondering why that detail played a factor. "And because somehow, she makes me *want* to stay."

Jerry nodded knowingly, but he continued. "And I'm still here because Elizabeth paints amazing pictures, and she told me she'd teach me how. And I like listening to her stories about her adventures as a reporter."

He was so lost in his thoughts his food was forgotten, and Jerry reached over to steal a piece of kiwi from his plate. He muffled his smile. "So," he asked, hoping his bribe had worked. "Are you going to out me?"

She sighed heavily, forcing her shoulders up and back with the force of her intake of breath, and then slowly down again with the release, as though he were asking a huge favor. "No, I suppose not." Glancing up at him from the corner of her eye, she winked. "It doesn't matter anyway, you know," she told him. "Katy wouldn't kick you out. She takes in stray people like old women take in cats."

"I'm learning that." He picked up a spoon and dug around in his baked beans before mumbling, "It's not her I'm worried about. Or rather, it *is* her, and the rest of you, that I'm worried about. If word gets out that I'm here, all hell will break loose."

"Don't worry," she assured him. "Your secret will remain safe with me."

She smiled at him with an odd look.

"What?" he asked self-consciously. Did he have ketchup on his chin? He took a swipe at his stubble, and she laughed.

"The interviews and pictures don't do you justice, you know. You are much more magnificent in person. Even with that awful haircut."

He rolled his eyes. "Good grief," was all he could answer. Normally, he would have smiled graciously and said thank you and escaped as soon as possible. But here, he realized, he didn't have to. She was teasing him, much like Livy did, and he appreciated it.

Katy looked over to him at that moment. A wide smile covered her face and knocked the breath from him. She was obviously glad that he was getting along so well with Jerry, after their strange introduction. He smiled back, pleased that he had once again made her happy.

Jerry eyed him suspiciously as she set down her cottage cheese, giving up all pretenses while she helped herself to more of his fruit. "Be careful, Caleb," she warned.

"What do you mean?" he asked, munching at another chip, stealing covert glances at his hostess. The sunset was doing incredible things to her hair.

"She has the potential to steal your heart," Jerry warned. "More than one traveler has become enamored."

He smiled ruefully. He wasn't going to be here long enough to fall for anyone. "I think I can handle myself," he said confidently.

"If you say so," Jerry shrugged. "I tried to warn you."

"I'll remember that at the wedding," he said sarcastically, adding a wink for good measure.

Jerry laughed. "I doubt it. You'll be too busy staring at Katy like you are now." His eyes immediately dropped to his plate. "But don't worry, I'll remind you."

"Whatever," he said, and he realized he was blushing. How embarrassing.

Jerry just laughed again.

The evening passed quickly. He helped Kyle and Elizabeth wash the dishes, which devolved into a water-fight. At first he was concerned about the older woman, but as he watched the young man get clobbered with a waterlogged sponge before the surprisingly spry and agile woman ducked out of the room, he realized this was a common occurrence. Apparently, Elizabeth was ruthless, and held no scruples when it came to water-fighting.

He had been properly warned.

But now that the household had settled into the routine of the night, he was growing restless as he sat on the couch, watching the stars overhead and the trail of the occasional cloud as it passed across the sky. He wasn't used to inactivity, and he wanted to move.

Jerry sat at the kitchen table with her laptop, working. Kyle had left for his physics class. Elizabeth was sprawled on a nearby couch reading and Ted had shut himself in his room with his cell phone. Katy had left for work.

Caleb realized he hadn't been able to walk down the street in so long that he couldn't remember the last time he'd done so. And he suddenly, desperately, wanted to. He jumped from his spot near the window and headed for the door, calling "I'll be back in a while," over his shoulder to Elizabeth.

He stopped on the porch, tossed his empty soda can in a convenient garbage pail and stretched his legs, looking at the neighborhood. It was quiet and dark. The children were in bed and the parents were headed there. A dog barked in the distance and, to his amazement, he heard a chicken clucking. At the end of the circular drive, the wooden Gilfrey's sign was lit up, and he wondered who Gilfrey was.

The rocks of the driveway crunched under his sneakers as he headed out, the trees around him casting dark shadows in the moonlight. There were no sidewalks to follow, but he stayed on the side of the road, in the dirt, and avoided the wildflowers when he could. Aimlessly he wandered, watching the shadows, the endless stars, and the bright moon.

The houses grew sparser, farther apart, the yards wider until the neighborhood was left behind altogether. He didn't turn back, following the dirt road he was on, loving the freedom and the soft night breeze.

Eventually he heard the gentle rush of water, and he realized that he'd arrived at the river. A wooden footbridge stretched across the expanse, and he walked to the center of it, took off his shoes, rolled up the bottom of his jeans and dangled his feet in the water. The river was cold but refreshing and he lay back on the bridge, pillowing his head with his hands while he trailed his toes in the gentle current.

He was outside, and there wasn't a flash bulb in sight. Peaceful serenity washed over him. He was truly content. The only thing that could make this moment more perfect was if Livy could be here with him. The thought made him pause.

Why not? If he couldn't go to his family, maybe he could bring them here. He doubted his parents would come on such short notice; they had work that they couldn't get away from. But why couldn't Livy visit? She'd love it here. She'd love Elizabeth, and Jerry and the paintings. Possibly Kyle and his guitar too, he thought wryly.

He'd ask Katy about it tomorrow; though he was pretty sure he already knew what the answer would be. That woman was genuine when she declared that "more was merrier." She let all the neighborhood children play on the jungle gym her grandfather had built for her and Ted when they were children. "We're not using it," she had said airily. "Why let it rot away, unused and unloved?"

As if the tree house and monkey bars had feelings that could be hurt. He smiled into the night, almost believing in the possibility.

****

Time passed slowly, the wispy clouds meandering across the expanse above him. He wasn't entirely positive, but he suspected that he'd drifted in and out of sleep a few times. Eventually though, his backside started to lose feeling and he knew it was time to go.

Reluctantly, he grabbed his shoes and socks and headed back. He wasn't ready to go back to the house yet, so he wandered mindlessly, not really paying attention to where he was going.

He vaguely noticed when the neighborhood grew thicker but it wasn't until he was standing in front of the vacant parking lot of the brightly lit Slurp-N-Go that he realized he actually had a destination in mind.

He balanced on each foot to wipe the mud off with his socks before slipping on his sneakers. He didn't bother to unroll his jeans, and stuffed the top of the dirty socks into his back pocket and headed into the store, pausing at the glass entrance.

Katy sat beside the register with a book spread out on the counter, a sheet of paper beside it and pencil poised. She was scowling at the book, her eyes shifting between the text and her paper. Abruptly, she slammed the pencil down and lightly banged her forehead on the paper once.

Caleb stood there for a moment, wondering if he should let her have her privacy. But then he saw the frustration and sadness in her eyes, and he was inside the store before he realized he'd made up his mind.

"Are you all right?" he asked, approaching her.

"No," she admitted, gesturing to her book. "No matter how many times I do this stupid problem, I get it wrong. And I get a different answer every time. And it's due tomorrow."

"What's the subject?" he asked, leaning against the counter and peering over to the book.

"Pre-algebra."

He cringed. Not his favorite subject, but he'd done decently enough in high school. It had been years since his honors calculus class, but maybe he could help her. "Let's see what the problem is."

****

Caleb leaned across the counter toward her looking adorably dorky. His black wavy hair framed his face, the edges of his long bangs scraping against the stubble on his chin. His white T-shirt was smeared with dirt and crumpled. His jeans were rolled up to his mid shins, and he was sockless in his sneakers. The dirty socks, which should have been on his feet, were dangling from a back pocket, trailing down his backside.

When he looked up at her with compassion in his eyes, the caffeine rush attacked her, as though the bottles of Jolt had been taken intravenously this time, so the carbonation could wreak havoc of its own free will.

He was offering to help her with her math, but how on earth was she going to concentrate? Taking a few deep breaths helped to calm the sensation, especially since he'd turned those eyes to her textbook, looking over the instructions and then back down to her paper.

"Here's your problem," he said, holding a hand out for her pencil and keeping his eyes on the algebra. She handed him the tool and watched as he pointed to the numbers with the pointy lead.

"See here? This is supposed to be a negative." He pointed to the problem in the book and back to her attempt.

Ugh, that didn't help. "Why?" she asked, feeling stupid.

"Because you can't subtract a positive from a negative," he explained. "This will actually make it easier for you. See, when you run across this, you need to change your 'minus' sign to a 'plus' sign, and change the second number to a negative. So what you are really doing is adding two negatives." He demonstrated, making the appropriate marks.

She looked at the paper, and then back to the textbook, then back to her paper. "So negative five minus two is not negative three, but really negative seven?"

"Exactly!" he said, smiling widely at her.

Groaning, she flopped onto her stool, burying her face in her arms on the counter.

"What's wrong?" he asked. "You got it now."

"Why couldn't they have explained it like you did?" she asked, frustrated. "Every single one of these problems is wrong!"

There was a moment of silence before he answered. "We could work on them together, if you want."

Raising her eyes to meet his, hope flared in her chest. "Are you sure?" she asked, not wanting to make him feel obligated. "It's late."

He shrugged. "It's not like I have any other plans tonight. Besides, I want to help. It's the least I could do. Please?"

He did. He really wanted to help her. And he wasn't laughing at her for being twenty-four years old, and stuck in a pre-algebra class. "Thank you," she told him, grabbing a tall stool and bringing it around to the front of the counter for him. "This is the second time I've taken this class," she admitted. "I can't afford to pay for it a third time."

"You're smart, Katy. I'm sure you can get this," he said with encouragement.

"No, Caleb, I'm not smart," she denied as she settled on her own stool behind the counter. "It's nice of you to say so, though. I graduated high school a year late, with a two point three grade average. For the last five years I've been working toward my AA, and I'm not even close. My goal is to get it before my thirtieth birthday."

She kept her eyes on her paper as she re-worked the next problem, too embarrassed to look up and see the horror, or pity, in his expression.

"Wow," he said quietly. "You are absolutely amazing."

Huh?

She raised her eyes to see Caleb looking at her with... admiration? She paused, lifting one eyebrow while the other scrunched downward slightly. "What?" she asked, feeling self-conscious. How on earth could he ascribe "brain challenged" as "amazing"?

"I don't know anybody else who wouldn't have given up by now," he told her. "You have no idea how much I admire your tenacity. I've never gone to college."

She ducked her head, looking back to her paper again. "I promised grandpa I wouldn't give up," she said. "So when I feel like quitting, I think of him sitting at the kitchen table, helping me with my homework every single night, and I can't let him down."

She raised her eyes again, meeting Caleb's, and shrugged. "Someday when I graduate, Grandpa will be sitting in the audience and whistling to me from me beyond the grave. So I keep re-taking these stupid classes!"

"What do you want to be when you grow up?"

"A historian."

Caleb paused. "Really?"

"I love history. I can *do* history. What I *can't* do is this junk!" she said, gesturing to her homework. "And English. I suck at English, too."

"You *can* do this", he assured. "You just did, remember? We'll just take it slow, all right? What's your next problem?"

For the rest of her shift, he sat on his side of the counter, quietly playing cards while she worked on the equations, patiently correcting her mistakes, and talking her through each problem until she understood it.

As the sun began to peek over the horizon, she was just finishing up her last problem and her boss walked through the front door, stopping to eye them. He cast a wary look at Caleb. "Do I know you?" he asked.

"This is Caleb," Katy introduced. "He's staying with us for a little bit. I'm trying to talk him into staying until the summer bash. He helped me with my math homework tonight. Caleb, this is Steven, owner and manager of Slurp-N-Go."

She started packing her books away, and closing out the register.

"Nice to meet you," Caleb said, politely holding out his hand. Steven took it, still wearing that weird look on his face.

"Nice to meet you too. Are you sure we've never met before?"

"No, I'm sure," Caleb promised. "I have one of those faces that people see everywhere."

He smiled at a personal joke, and Katy wondered what it was.

"Huh," her boss said, still unconvinced. "Well, anyway," he said, back to business, "how'd it go last night?"

What he meant was sales. "Ten or eleven cars stopped for gas," which was the real reason he kept the store open all night, "and I sold a deck of cards, two diet colas and a candy bar."

He smiled. "Sales are picking up!" he declared happily.

She didn't have the heart to tell him that her tutor was his lone customer. "Goodnight, Steven," she answered.

Caleb grabbed her bag from her and held the door open. "Thank you," she said, surprised. "You don't need to do that."

He laughed. "Yes I do. My mother would find out

somehow, and I don't want to sit through another one of her lectures."

He smiled at her, and Katy embraced the caffeine rush while plotting ways to keep him in town as long as possible. But for now, he was going to walk her home, and the morning sunrise had never been quite as breathtaking.

Chapter Four

Caleb sat in the driver's seat of his car, drumming his fingers against the steering wheel in time to the music, humming softly to himself and watching the college students as they traveled to their various destinations across campus, conducting research for work. It was fun to people-watch. He studied their body movements, their mannerisms, their tics.

He had a wide assortment of humanity to engross himself in. Because it was a community college, every age was represented. The set of their feet and body as they stood, the way their faces and mouths moved as they talked, the way they gestured with their hands, the movement of their eyes—it all fascinated him. He loved to watch people, and he caught himself mimicking them from his hiding spot behind his tinted windows and laughed ruefully. When he was a kid, sometimes he'd even practice in front of a mirror, to get just the right inflection.

The classroom door nearest his car opened and a stream of young adults began to emerge. He watched each of them until Katy finally stepped into the sunshine, and he carefully judged her mood. She'd been so nervous walking into class because there was a test today. But her face was a mask, and he couldn't decide how well she'd done. Slowly she approached his car, opened the passenger side and slid in.

"Well?" he asked anxiously. "How'd it go? How'd you do?" He leaned in her direction, nervous for her.

Katy's entire face lit up into sunshine and she smiled wide, eyes sparkling, as she threw her arms around his neck, squealing with glee. She pecked his scruffy cheek with a light smooch before hugging him tighter in her enthusiasm.

"Thank you!" she declared. "Thank you, thank you, thank you!"

He was being choked, and the position was awkward, his legs trapped under the steering wheel as his body was being pulled closer to the passenger seat, but he couldn't help but laugh. It came out a strangled gurgle. "So you did well," he said with a voice changed in octave by her hold on his neck.

He couldn't return the hug; her seat was obstructing access on one side, so he patted her on the back with his left hand. She released him at last and leaned away, resting her back on the passenger door, still facing him, still smiling. "Yes I did. I think I may have even gotten a B! At the very least a C plus, I'm sure of it. And it's all because of you!"

"No it wasn't," he told her, shaking his head as he pulled out of the parking lot. "I wasn't in there taking that test with you. You did it all on your own."

"Caleb, you stayed up all night with me helping me to study. You gave me a ride to class, even though I could have taken the bus this morning, just so I could sleep a little. Trust me, you made all the difference."

"There was no reason for you to take a bus six hours before class started when I have a perfectly good vehicle doing nothing at all," he argued.

"I do it twice every week," she reminded him.

"Well, if I was here twice every week, I'd give you a ride," he told her as he spotted an ice cream drive-through. Impulsively, recklessly, he pulled in.

"What do you like?" he asked as they inched up to the ordering board. "My treat. We're going to celebrate your good score."

"Caleb, I don't know," she said hesitantly. "You don't need to buy me ice-cream, you're out of work—"

"I'm between jobs, Katy, there's a difference," he told her, wanting to laugh but holding it in. Katy was possibly the first woman to ever ask him if he could afford something. "Trust me, ice-cream isn't a problem. I *want* to buy you ice-cream. I *want* to celebrate with you. Don't take that away from me," he said, turning the tables on her.

It worked.

"Well, if you're sure...."

"I'm sure. This isn't going to bankrupt me. What do you want? Anything."

Her face became excited as she scanned the board, and he wondered how long it had been since she'd indulged in something so simple.

"I would like..." she paused, making sure she read everything. Cars started pulling up behind them, and the employee asked for a second time if they were ready yet, their politeness edging on panicky. "... I think I would like a Chocolate Malt, extra thick, extra chocolaty." Her eyes darted to him. "Is that ok?"

He couldn't help it, he did laugh that time and assured her that yes, he could afford the "extra thick" and the "extra chocolate."

She looked at him weirdly when he ordered their treats in a different timbre of voice than his natural tone, and when he kept his head lowered and hair covering his face as much as possible while paying for and retrieving their order through the window. But she didn't comment.

After pulling away, he tapped the tip of his strawberry milkshake against the top of her malt. "To high scores on tests," he said. "This one, and the ones in the future."

She smiled at him and took a swig of her drink.

He nearly drove off the road, he was so absorbed in watching the play of emotions cross her face as she sucked the ice cream through the straw and then so obviously took delight in the flavors. Her eyes closed in ecstasy and she sighed softly. The way her mouth moved, he could picture her rolling the drink over her tongue, savoring the sensations before swallowing and taking another pull.

He gripped the steering wheel so hard his knuckles turned white, and forced himself to keep his eyes on the road so he wouldn't kill them. Still, he could see her out of the corner of his eye, enjoying that chocolate malt like it was the very last one she would ever be granted, and every time she lifted that straw to her mouth, he had to remind himself to breathe.

She looked so *happy*. She almost always looked happy, but you'd think he'd just given her a diamond necklace or something. And he loved the fact, took pride in the fact, that he was the one who brought her that moment of joy... with something as silly as an ice-cream.

Watching her drink was possibly one of the best things he'd ever done in his life, and he was grateful she took her time about it.

"Thank you so much, Caleb. I haven't had one of these in a very long time," she told him at last, lifting her cup slightly.

"It was my pleasure." Really. It was.

They didn't talk a great deal on the way home, but the silence was companionable.

It wasn't until a few days later that the subject of his financial situation arose again, with a completely different person.

Stretched out on his bed listening to music on his mp3 player with the door closed, eyes closed, his ankles crossed, he relived the car ride in his thoughts while simultaneously considering going for

39

a nighttime swim in the river. Unfortunately, a harsh knocking on the door shattered his concentration.

Sitting up, he pulled the headphones off and called out. "Come on in." He wondered what he could have done to whom to earn that kind of knock, when Jerry stalked in.

She managed to look elegantly casual in her designer jeans and blouse. Her hair was in her French braid and her make-up still looked perfect. But she was... miffed... about something, and apparently Caleb was the culprit.

He started reviewing sins that Livy used to complain about, but he couldn't think of anything he had transgressed with here. He diligently used the "man bathroom," so he wasn't guilty of leaving the toilet seat up, or leaving beard hair on the sink. He hadn't even shaved in four days. He helped wash the dishes, and didn't even break any. He hadn't left dirty clothes or trash anywhere....

"What is this?" she asked stiffly, raising a fist with green paper jutting out of the top.

Oh, that. Was that all?

"It looks like money," he answered innocently.

She rolled her eyes and stepped into the room, thwapping him with the money. "All right, smart mouth. Would you like to explain why the cookie jar has five hundred and seventy three dollars in it, when it's never gotten above thirty?"

He shrugged. "It procreated?"

She smacked his shoulder with the back of her hand this time, but she laughed despite her ire. Plopping next to him on the bed, she held the wad of cash out to him. "Seriously, Caleb. We can't take this. It's too much."

He shook his head, pulling up his knees to rest his elbows on. "No it's not, Jerry. It's grocery money and rent."

She sighed. "Did you bother to count this before you stuffed it in?"

He shrugged, and she rolled her eyes. "You're as bad with money as she is," she groaned, and he automatically knew which "she" was being referred to.

"You can't tell me that Katy can't use it," he answered. "I don't need it. And besides, I'm mooching off you guys until the summer bash thing."

"So you *are* going to stay that long?" she asked, getting diverted momentarily.

Playing with his mp3 player he nodded. "Yeah, she wants me to."

"And what Katy wants, Katy gets," Jerry mused with a smile.

One side of his mouth lifted. "How can a person tell her 'no' when it's so much fun to tell her 'yes'?"

"It's only been a handful of days, Caleb, and you're already lost," she told him, her voice low and compassionate.

He shrugged, not denying it this time. "It's only a crush, Jerry. I'll get over it."

She paused, looking at compassionately, mentally calculating something. At last she answered. "Sure, Caleb. You'll be gone soon, back to the real world, and this will be a just a fantastic dream."

The thought depressed him and he frowned.

"About this money," she said, holding up the cash again. "You can't put any more money in the cookie jar."

He narrowed his eyes, snapped his jaw shut and turned his gaze to the darkened window beside him, frustrated and annoyed by the order. "I'm not trying to buy her friendship."

"I know," she told him, laying a hand on his leg and patting it, trying to placate him. There was a moment of silence before she laughed ruefully.

His head snapped around, upset that she would find his discomfort funny. But she patted his leg again. "I'm just happy to meet the real you," she explained. "They," she said, referring to the ubiquitous paparazzi, "know all about your charm, your magnetism, your really hot body. But they have no idea that you are happiest when you are helping other people."

He scrunched his mouth, his eyes narrowing, denying her claim.

"No, I've seen it. You are just like Katy—"

"No one is like Katy," he denied.

"—in the fact that you love people. You love to listen to Elizabeth's stories and paint pictures with her. You give me fruit, and let me pretend that I'm sticking to my ridiculous diet. You listen to Kyle play his guitar and listen to him talk about airplanes in technical terms that go above your head. And you look at pictures of Ted's wife and daughter and actually appear to enjoy it."

He shrugged. "I like you guys."

"That's my point, Caleb." He still didn't "get" her point, and the look on his face must have revealed that to her. "I guess what I'm saying is that I like you. As a person. You're a great guy."

"Thanks," he said as the blood rushed through his face. "But I'm still not allowed to pay anymore into the cookie jar?"

She paused, looking at him seriously. "If you're here past the bash, we'll negotiate."

He couldn't stop the slow smile from creeping across his face, and Jerry laughed at him, getting up off the bed.

"I've got work to do," she said.

He was lonely when she left. Elizabeth and Ted had retired for the evening, Kyle was on a date and Katy at work. Rummaging through the suitcase he had lugged up to his room days ago, he located his cutoff jean shorts and a T-shirt and changed quickly. Throwing on his sneakers without socks, he made his way to the kitchen long enough to tell Jerry he was going for a swim before heading out of the house.

As with the previous nights, he stood on the porch for a few minutes, stretching his legs and listening to the sounds of the sleeping neighborhood. The chicken was clucking, the crickets chirping, and he detected a low hum from the light on the Gilfrey sign. A warm breeze picked up, whooshing through the trees. Livy would like it here. It was too bad summer camp started in a few days.

He breathed in deeply, pulling the scent and the vibrancy of the evening inside himself. He felt good. He took his time walking to the river, enjoying the dark shadows and the stars overhead. When he reached the inlet of the river Elizabeth had told him about, he stripped off his shirt and shoes and jumped inside.

For a moment, he thought he was going to suffer a heart attack and die, the water was so cold. But after a few moments, he acclimated. The current was like velvet over his skin, refreshing and relaxing. He splashed and floated and cannon-balled for a while, until his energy started to wane. It was fun, but not satisfying. Something was missing.

So he pulled himself out, and started wandering again. And somehow, despite his resolve not to, he ended up in the vacant parking lot of the Slurp-N-Go again, as he had all the other nights. He sighed, frustrated with himself. Then he walked into the store.

****

Katy forced herself to breathe as she deftly hid her book under the counter, smiling up at Caleb while he gooshed his way over to her. He was soggy, and his shoes made squishy sounds as he walked,

43

but he was here.

"Hey," she greeted.

"Hey," he said, looking at her intently through his disheveled hair. He leaned on the counter, and let his gaze drift down to where her hands were. "Whatchya reading?"

Oh, this was so embarrassing. Reluctantly, she pulled the book from its hiding place and presented it to him. "It's *The Alaria Chronicles*," she told him.

"What's it about?" he asked, flipping the book over in his hands, looking at it without reading the synopsis.

"It's about a boy and a girl who are teamed up as children to fight an invading race of giant Ticks that are killing all the humans. They grow up warriors, and it's about their teamwork and... well... it's their love story." She said the last part defiantly, daring him to make fun of her.

"Warriors, huh?" he asked. "Is there a lot of action?"

"In parts," she answered.

"Why don't you read it to me?" he asked.

Was he kidding? She looked up at him, and his eyes were searching hers, lonely. He would do anything for companionship right now; even listen to a fluffy scifi-chick book. Her heart melted, and she grabbed the stool he'd used the previous nights and carted it around the counter for him before returning to her post.

"I'm warning you," she told him. "I'm a very slow reader. That's one of the reasons I'm so lousy at school."

"No problem," he assured her, getting comfortable on his now-familiar perch. "How about you read a chapter, and then I'll read a chapter."

"Are you sure about this?" she asked. "We could just talk, you know. Or play cards."

"No, really. Let's read."

And so they did. At first, she was self-conscious with her slow reading, tripping over words and having to sound some out. But he listened intently, with all apparent engrossment, and as she relaxed it started to come easier. The first chapter took an hour, and then he took over.

Taking the book from her outstretched hand, Caleb exaggerated his movements as he adjusted on his bar stool, supposedly finding the most comfortable position, cleared his throat and searched the pages for chapter two. After finding the appropriate passage, he straightened an imaginary pair of glasses on his nose and pulled the book backward and forward a couple of times, as though trying to manually adjust the focus.

Katy rolled her eyes and laughed. "Will you just get on with it?"

He glanced up with a smile, causing her heart to stop beating briefly. He cleared his throat one last time as he plopped his elbows onto her counters and began.

"Andrea threw herself face first onto her mattress and covered her head with her pillow before screaming. She was so sick and tired of being in love with her best friend, her assigned partner for the last five years. She didn't want to love him. She'd tried for the last three years to stop herself from loving him. But it was pointless. She was hopelessly, pathetically in love with a man who didn't love her back. Well... not like *that*."

Katy wasn't sure what to expect before he'd started. Derision maybe. Jokes, perhaps, at the expense of the fictional teenagers who were on the verge of national war and personal love. But as his voice floated through the store, strong and confident, there was only the story and respect for the young woman and her plight.

"...And it didn't even faze her when Kevin had

gotten sick and thrown up on her last month, and then used her favorite headscarf to try to clean up the mess."

Caleb stopped his reading to laugh heartily as he smacked his forehead. "That kid needs to get a clue."

"Give the guy a break," she said, defending the young man even though she was chuckling too. "Maybe it came on suddenly and he couldn't move fast enough to miss her."

"Ok, accidents happen," he relented. "But they've been paired up together for five years now. Five." Caleb punctuated his point by holding up a hand with his fingers spread. "He should know by now how important Andrea's 'pretties' are to her." He shook his head with disgust. "I've only known her for an hour, and even I would know better than to grab *any* of her scarves, let alone her favorite, to wipe up my vomit. Not only was he risking another broken nose, that is not the way to get the woman you adore to love you."

"But he doesn't adore her yet," Katy argued. "He probably used the scarf because all 'pretties' as you called them, really irritate him. And she only broke his nose on accident."

"Yeah, all four times." Her narrator shook his head. "But aside from that, he's had a crush on her since before their 'Joining,' back when they were eleven, despite all the personal injury she causes him."

"Uh huh," she said with disbelief. Were they reading the same story? Did he listen at all to the entire first chapter? "That's why he was so mean to her all that time before the whole 'Confrontation With the Pure Bloods' incident? Because he had a crush on her?"

And so the good-natured argument ensued for ten minutes over motivations and the fact that the characters were only sixteen. When Caleb picked up the book and started reading again, Katy smiled.

She couldn't remember the last time she'd been so entertained.

Chapter Five

Two weeks later, Caleb found himself sitting on the roof of the backyard tree house next to Ted, drinking a cold cream soda. They were silent, taking a break from the early evening's work of patching a hole, and he wondered why the man had asked for his help. Not that he minded, but Ted was more than capable of doing the work on his own. In fact, Caleb had a suspicion that his "help" had been more problematic than beneficial.

Ted shifted beside him and coughed softly. "I know who you are," he finally said.

Caleb choked on his drink, sputtering and spilling syrupy liquid down his shirt.

"How?" he asked, his voice rough. "How long?"

"I have a fifteen year old daughter." The farmer chuckled. "Your posters are plastered all over her bedroom. I knew the moment you stepped out of your car that first night three weeks ago."

Caleb thought about that for a few minutes. "Then why—"

"It's none of my business. I figure if you're using a different name, you're lookin' for some anonymity. But we have a problem. My wife and daughter are comin' to the summer bash this weekend and I can promise, Emily *will* recognize you." Ted smiled ruefully. "I didn't say anything before this because I didn't realize it was going to be an issue. I didn't know you'd be here this long."

"So I need to go," Caleb observed, his stomach clenching at the thought.

"No one's kicking you out," Ted assured. "But I've got to tell my daughter *something*. She'll be mad, but I can make her promise not to tell anyone you're here, or that she met you, at least until you're gone. Bragging rights, you know. She'd be the envy of all her friends." He paused. "She's a good kid, she'll keep her promises. But I'd want to tell her ahead of time, before she meets you. It might cut down on some of the theatrics, also, if she's pre-warned."

Caleb thought about the options for a moment. Katy's cousin was a good man, and he was a good judge of character. If he said his daughter could keep a secret, could he trust him? He thought about leaving early and a dull pain gripped his chest. No. He would keep his promise to Katy.

"Can I meet her without an audience?" he asked nervously.

"You mean without Katy or Elizabeth around?"

"Yeah," he affirmed. That was precisely what he meant.

Ted nodded. "We can arrange that."

"Is there anything I can bribe her with?" Caleb asked, not above underhanded tactics. "Something to lessen the blow of not being able to brag right away?"

The father laughed. "Dance with her once, and let her take a picture of it," was the answer. "She will have proof after you're gone, and all her friends will be green with envy."

Caleb smiled. That was easy enough. "No problem. I would love to dance with her. We can take a whole photo album of pictures."

A voice called from the kitchen door, interrupting their conversation. "Ted!" Elizabeth called. "Can you send Caleb in here? I want to show him something"

"No problem!" Ted called back. "He'll be there in

a minute!" He lowered his voice. "They'll be getting into town tomorrow evening. We can meet you at the river, if that's all right."

"That's fine," Caleb answered, climbing down the rope ladder then heading toward the kitchen. He forced his mind to turn toward the artist, refusing to dwell on Emily.

When he stepped into the brightly lit room, he was greeted by the sight of Elizabeth dancing in the middle of the kitchen with a giant purple apron tied around her body, bowls and various ingredients spread all over the kitchen table. There was barely enough room for Jerry, who sat diligently typing at her laptop, casting him glances and fighting a smile. Kyle sat in a window seat nearby, serenading them with his guitar.

The tune was catchy, and he couldn't help himself. Snatching Elizabeth up, he twirled her around and led her across the kitchen floor, Fred Astair and Ginger Rogers style. The older woman giggled happily, following his lead easily.

"You are really good at this!" she exclaimed.

"I had to learn for a role I did once," he explained.

"*Fifth Moonless Night*," Jerry mumbled, not looking up from her work.

"What was that, dear?" Elizabeth asked as they twirled past.

"I said it looks like it's going to be a moonless night," Jerry clarified, still working at her laptop.

"So what did you want to show me?" Caleb asked, winking at Jerry.

"She's going to teach you how to bake," Kyle spoke up from his corner of the kitchen. "I was a hopeless failure at it, so she's trying you now." He was smiling indulgently, enjoying the show, his fingers still adeptly plucking out their tune.

They swung to a stop, in front of the table again,

and Caleb eyed the contents warily. "I don't know how to bake, Lizzie."

"Lizzie?" she asked with a delighted smile, momentarily diverted from her mission. But before he could comment, she remembered her purpose for calling him inside. "Have you ever tried?" she asked.

"Well, no," he admitted.

"Then you don't know if you can or can't, don't you? We're making peanut butter cookies," she told him enticingly. When he looked at her doubtfully, her eyes narrowed, and she pulled out the big guns. "This is Katy's favorite recipe."

Ugh, she just had to go there, didn't she? They all knew that he spent every night, all night, at work with her. They all knew that he walked her home every morning. And this morning, Elizabeth had come out of the house to see him holding Katy's hand as they climbed the porch steps.

The old woman fought dirty. Sighing, he picked up a spoon. "All right, woman. Teach me. But I take no responsibility for the results, should the house burn down."

She smiled up at him, her eyes twinkling. His heart softened and realized that even if the cookies came out disgusting, it was worth putting forth the effort, just to make Elizabeth happy.

****

Caleb walked into the store with flour in his hair, a goofy smile on his face and a plastic-wrapped plate in his hands. He looked so proud of himself.

"What do you have there?" Katy asked, intrigued, as he sauntered over to the counter.

He wiggled his eyebrows at her and smiled warmly. "Peanut butter cookies," he said, laying the plate down on the glass in front of her, leaning in close and pinning her with those dark eyes of his. Elizabeth had made the comparison to Hershey's chocolate, and at this close range, Katy could corroborate that he definitely had candy-bar eyes. She barely registered when he continued his explanation. "Elizabeth says they are your favorite."

"These were made from her secret recipe? And you brought them for me?" she asked breathlessly, touched by his kindness.

"I *made* them for you." He wiggled his eyebrows again. After all this time in his company, Katy had figured the novelty of his presence would wane, that the caffeine/carbonation rush would dim with time and grow a little flat, like the soda, but it didn't.

Instead, it seemed like every single day he cranked it up a notch. As with the Jolt she'd drunk every day in her teen years, she was addicted. And like the summer she'd sworn off soda, when Caleb left, she would suffer serious withdrawals. But she couldn't help herself; she was not going to send him away. He would have to leave of his own free will.

Even then, she might fight him. She'd been fighting his departure every day.

"Thank you," she finally stammered, realizing that she'd been staring at him. And then, because he seemed to like it, she leaned over and kissed his cheek. Well, she leaned over and kissed where his cheek would have been, if the scraggily beard hadn't been in the way.

She was right about his hair color; it was not midnight black naturally. His beard was a weird combination of blond, brown and auburn, and the roots of his hair, which were just beginning to show, matched his facial hair. She wondered what he looked like when he wasn't on vacation.

"You're welcome," he said, smiling at her warmly.

She reached up and ruffled his hair in an attempt to clear off the flour, but he ducked out of the way, laughing. Retrieving and paying for a medium-sized jug of milk, he plopped down on his stool and pulled out a deck of cards. They'd finished another book last night, and had occupied the remaining hours of her shift with a brutal game of rummy. Apparently, he wanted a rematch.

"You're just going to lose again," she warned him, climbing onto her stool and peeling back the plastic wrap from the plate. "You don't have a chance of winning."

"Oh really?" he said, shuffling the cards meticulously. "You think you're all that, huh?"

"I *am* all that," she said confidently, tugging the plastic security tab off the milk and gesturing for him to deal already.

"I bet you two cookies that I win the first hand," he challenged, his elbows resting on the table, his eyes daring her.

"That's no fair!" she protested. "They are already my cookies!" She narrowed her eyes. "Unless you're going to be a 'taker-backer.'"

He paused, thinking for a second before he started dealing the cards. "Ok, you have a point," he said. "If I win, you have to make another one of those lemon meringue pies you served yesterday. If you win the game, I have to take you for another extra-thick, extra-chocolaty Chocolate Malt."

He lifted his eyes toward her, and she saw a gleam in them she didn't understand. But the bet seemed fair. "Ok," she said at last, wondering what his angle was when he smiled triumphantly. He was laughing on the inside about something. What did she miss?

The cards were dealt and she picked up her hand, sorting them by the various numbers and suits. Absently, she picked up a cookie and plopped it whole into her mouth, instantly melting. Oh, he'd done a fantastic job.

Elizabeth must have talked him through every step of the baking process, because it was perfect.

The cookie was moist and chewy, but slightly crumbly, and as it filled every crevice of her mouth, the flavors seemed to explode. Chewing was heavenly.

She opened her eyes to look at her cards and saw Caleb sitting across from her, staring. He was perfectly still, without even the rise and fall of his chest.

How humiliating. She probably looked so disgusting with her mouth stuffed completely full, chewing on her cookie like a cow chewing its cud. And she'd been rude, too. Sheepishly she swallowed two or three times to get all the cookie down, and then held one out in his direction.

"They are *really*, really good," she told him as he gulped and accepted her offering. "Thank you," she added.

And then she committed another social blunder. Without thinking about it, she lifted the carton of milk to her mouth and chugged. About three guzzling swallows in, her eyes got wide, and she dropped the container back to the counter, embarrassed, wondering what he thought of her really bad manners.

Before her fingers completely separated from the milk, his wrapped around it from the other side, and he absently lifted the jug to his mouth and drank as he studied his cards.

She smiled at him helplessly and wondered if it was possible to fall in love in two weeks. He was so patient and kind and... wonderful. And he drank from the jug. Who couldn't love a man who didn't mind sharing cooties?

"So," he asked her conversationally as he waited for her to decide whether to pick up from the discard pile, or draw. "Who's Gilfrey?"

"Gilfrey is my great grandmother's maiden name," she told him, drawing and discarding. He picked up her discard and she scowled at him. He ignored her. "She ran it as a boarding house for a while, back in the day."

"Whose handprints are in the hallway?" he asked.

"Mostly my mother's and my aunts. A bunch are mine. Some are Ted's. When Grandpa took me in after my folks' car crash, one of the first things he did was get my handprints on the walls. Whenever Ted came to stay over the summer, his prints went up as well."

"How old were you?" Caleb asked softly.

"Five," she answered. "Poor Grandpa, dealing with a little girl all by himself like that. But we helped each other. We needed each other."

"He sounds like a really great guy," her card partner said.

"He was fantastic," she said, feeling nostalgic. "He sat through more tea-parties and fairy-stories than any man should have to endure."

"I'll bet you he loved every minute of it," Caleb told her.

She laughed. "I remember the first time he took me and Ted fishing together. He showed me how to bait the hook and how to cast. Since Ted is eleven years older than me, he was already a teenager and gone tons of times with him. When I grossed out over the worm and tripped over his tackle-box, Grandpa just helped me clean up the mess, and kissed my hair.

"He taught me how to swim and how to tie my shoes and how to make snowballs and meatballs and curveballs."

"And he taught you how to love life and the people around you," Caleb observed. "I wish I could have known him."

"Me too," Katy said softly. "I think he would have really liked you."

Caleb smiled at her, warmly at first, and then mischievously. "Rummy," he declared, pulling a card from the discard pile and placing his entire hand on the table.

She sucked her tongue against her teeth for a second, eyeing him shrewdly. "Oh, so it's like that, is it?"

"Lemon meringue pie is on the table, sweetheart. It is very much like that."

"Ok, gloves are off," she declared. "You won't win again tonight."

He laughed, daring her.

She raised an eyebrow and began to shuffle. "So now it's your turn. Tell me about your family."

"Trying to distract me?" he asked, grabbing a cookie and munching.

"With everything in my arsenal," Katy confirmed. "Tell all."

She began to deal the cards, and he picked up each one, sorting them. His eyes were distant, though. He began to tell her about his sister Livy, and his parents. She listened, entranced. The love for his family shone on his face. He was proud of his sister, and how she was going to be a biochemical engineer someday.

As the evening progressed, the cookies and milk disappeared and the scores mounted. They fought a good battle—sometimes she was in the lead, sometimes he was until at last, she threw down her cards triumphantly. Katy jumped from her stool, arms in the air above her in a victory "V" and shimmied a little dance.

With a huge smile on his face, he folded up his massive wad of cards without revealing his hand, and shuffled the deck together. "All right, you win this round," he relented graciously. "I owe you one chocolate malt, payment due this Monday when I take you to class."

Her heart stopped. He wasn't going to leave immediately after the summer bash.

Suddenly, her victory dance took on a whole new meaning.

Chapter Six

Caleb lay back on his bed, listening to music and feeling completely relaxed. He was in jeans and his favorite black T-shirt, so old he was worried it would disintegrate in the dryer one of these days. It was bliss to not shave, though his hair was getting annoying. He needed the camouflage and didn't dare cut it. In a few minutes, he'd have to go meet Emily and play Movie Star again, but for now, he could just be himself.

"All right, loverboy. Do you care to explain yourself? What's your game?"

He looked up from his perch on his bed to his doorway in confusion.

Jerry stood in the entrance, still dressed in her work clothes, briefcase in one hand, her purse slung over her shoulder.

He peeled the headphones from his ear. "I'm not guilty this time," he defended himself. "I haven't put anything else in the cookie jar, I swear."

She drew a magazine from behind her where she'd been hiding it and threw it on his bed, expertly landing it next to his thigh.

Slowly, he picked the rag up and glanced at the cover. "DERRICK NELSON TAKES SECRET VACATION AT THE BEACH WITH VERONICA DEWITT!!" shouted their headline, and then in smaller letters "'They are so cute together!' declares inside source."

Under the bold lettering were several pictures of a very recognizable, sans obnoxious haircut and beard, Derrick Nelson. He was frolicking because, quite honestly that was the most accurate word to describe what he was doing, with superstar Veronica DeWitt over the sand and surf. He was in swim trunks, she in a bikini, and in a few pictures, they were tightly embraced.

Caleb froze for a second before opening the magazine and scanning the article, studying each of the pictures. A slow, jubilant smile lit up his face and he began laughing. "God bless you, Abigail! I am going to give you a raise!"

He started to reach to his nightstand for his cell phone, but Jerry apparently wasn't going to let him get away with prevarication. "How old are those pictures?" she demanded. "And are you involved with Veronica DeWitt? Because so help me, if you are playing some sort of sick game here for your amusement, I will—"

"That's not me," Caleb told her calmly, his phone in his hand now. "And my guess is that those pictures were taken last week."

Jerry didn't believe him, and she let her expression tell him so.

"That's Frank Thermopolis, my body double," he told her, his eyes level with hers, smiling ridiculously. "Do you see a single clear picture in that entire collection?"

Warily, Jerry picked up the magazine and looked more closely. One by one, she studied the pictures and he knew that she was finally seeing what he did. Yes, there were several crystal clear pictures, but they were all from an angle, the side, behind, or a distance. The ones from the front always had his face partially obscured by Veronica, or were slightly grainy.

"And to answer your question, no, Veronica and I are not involved," he told her, pushing a button on his cell phone. "She's repaying a favor she owes me."

He motioned for Jerry to sit down on the bed, and she followed his direction, obviously still leery. "Abigail, my love!" Caleb called into the phone happily, hitting the speakerphone button.

The woman on the other end of the line was laughing. "I thought that might make you come out of the woodwork," she told him. "Todd is at a loose end over here. How do you expect him to do his job if you insist on running out on us like that?"

"Tell your husband that I am fine," Caleb assured his manager. He looked up at Jerry and winked at her. She was sitting in front of him frowning slightly, but she was softening.

"That diversion is only going to work for so long, you know. That psychotic fan of yours is enraged that you deigned to disappear into to the woodwork without consulting her first. Todd is concerned your stunt might push her into something more drastic than writing possessive, vaguely threatening letters." She paused momentarily. "Where are you, Derrick?"

"At the end of the rainbow," he answered and he heard her groan.

"You make it hard for a woman to do her job. And her husband gets really cranky when the man he's supposed to be guarding goes AWOL. Why hire the man to be your security specialist if you're going to sneak out on him?"

"You are a pillar of strength for putting up with me," he declared. "Tell Mr. Betencorp to give you a raise. That vacation leak was pure genius."

"You gave me a raise last month, remember?" she told him laughingly.

"That was Todd," he corrected.

"Same thing," she insisted. "I'll save your accountant the heartache and wait a month."

"Whatever you want," he told her. "When do I need to be in Chicago?"

"On the twenty third," she told him. "I need to know where to book the flight out from, Derrick."

He knew he could trust her. In two and a half years, she'd never once given him a reason to doubt her integrity or loyalty. But he didn't want to tell her. He didn't want to tell anyone. He was living in some remarkable fairy tale, and he had the irrational feeling that saying the words would make the whole thing pop like a bubble, and he'd be back in a hotel room, alone, waiting for his bodyguards to escort him to dinner while people hid in the shadows watching him.

"I'll book my own flight," he told her. "Meet me in Chicago on the twenty second. You and Todd take a vacation. Go anywhere you want, my treat."

She sighed, frustrated. "At least answer your phone when I call," she insisted.

He sighed dramatically. "All right, all right. Jeez, you sound like my mom."

"You haven't been calling your mom?" Abigail asked in surprise. "Are you sure you're all right, Derrick?"

"I'm fine," he said. "And I was speaking theoretically. I've been calling my mom regularly, I promise."

Jerry looked at him with an eyebrow raised, but he ignored her.

"Take care of yourself, kid."

"Don't worry about it, Abigail," he said. "I'm fine."

"It's my job to worry about it, that's what you pay me for, remember?" She sounded mercenary, but she really did care, and it touched his heart, making him feel guilty for ignoring her for so long. "But you sound good," she continued. "I haven't heard you this... relaxed in a very long time. It's nice.

"I'm happy," he told her. "Tell Todd 'hi' for me, and I'll see ya'll later this month." He hung up and looked at Jerry. "Do you have any more questions?"

She thought about it for a second. "None that are any of my business," she decided. "So you'll be here for three more weeks," she noted, standing up and heading for his door.

He shrugged, looking down and flipping his cell phone in his hands. "I'd like to be."

"Good," Jerry answered, smiling at him before walking out and heading for her room.

Looking at the clock, he realized it was time to rendezvous with Ted, his wife and Emily. For the first time in two weeks, he took the time to dress carefully. He changed into a newer... ish... black button-down shirt and tried to comb his hair. The experience was painful, since he hadn't bothered combing it all week. After his daily showers, he'd run the towel over his hair and let it dry in wavy tangles.

When the mop was in some semblance of control, he carefully laced his black boots before finally heading out. He almost shaved. He would have, if he didn't need his beard to get him through his first foray into public tomorrow. Emily was a fan, and she was looking forward to meeting someone that she admired and cared about. She deserved to be treated with respect. He hoped she wouldn't be too disappointed. He'd make it up to her later somehow.

The walk was familiar now, and he made his way easily to the footbridge. He was a few minutes early, so he leaned on the railing, watching the reflections of the setting sun on the water. The swirl beneath him was a kaleidoscope colors, turbulent and unrelenting.

At last, Ted's battered truck pulled up and parked near the bridge. Everything was still for a few minutes, and Caleb began to wonder if everyone was all right.

Finally, both doors opened, and the family climbed out.

****

The girl stared at him doubtfully as he walked toward her, giving him hope that his new appearance altered his identity well... until she froze. Inwardly, he sighed. This was so embarrassing. But he owed her gratitude, so he smiled.

"Hello, Emily," he greeted. He held out his hand and when she pushed hers forward slightly, he grasped it in both of his and shook gently. "It's good to meet you. Your father has told me a lot about you."

She was a good kid, from all reports, and she had kind eyes. She stared at him momentarily, her mouth opening and closing slightly.

"I...I..." she began, and he saw the horror in her eyes.

His smile didn't waver; he still felt the same way every time he ran into Angelina Jolie. "Hey, there's a great view of the sunset on the water over on the footbridge that I'll bet you'd love. I was looking at it before you got here. Why don't you come check it out?"

He had to get her comfortable, or this would be a very long weekend indeed. He casually flung his arm around her shoulders and led in the right direction. Their footsteps made hollow thunking noises as they stepped over the wooden structure, and he continued, trying to put her at ease. "I come out here most nights to look at the stars. It's incredible."

He stopped in the middle of the bridge, and turned her to face the water, letting go of her shoulders and resting his hands on the railing. "Check it out," he said pointing down. "I wish you could have seen it a few minutes ago, it was beautiful, but a lot of the light has gone."

Emily looked at the water and her response was instantaneous. "Wow," she said breathlessly, as her eyes soaked in the scene before them, and he felt pleased that he could share this with her, show her beauty.

They stood side by side for a few minutes, watching the water and the light as it faded. "So I hear you're a good swimmer," he said, trying to pull her from her silence. Emily cringed, but he continued on anyway. "How did the swim meet go yesterday?"

"Um, I got first in the fifty meter relay," she said, glancing up at him. He had been watching the river, but he felt fatherly triumph and didn't try to hide his excitement for her.

"Great job!" he exclaimed, holding his hand up for a high-five. She smacked his hand, looking proud of her accomplishment. "Your dad is a really great guy," he said, indicating to the shoreline with a nod of his head.

"Yeah, he can be okay," Emily relented, with a curiously rebellious look in her eyes as she darted them to her father.

"So I keep hearing wonderful things about this summer bash that we're all going to tomorrow," he said. "What's so great about it? What's your favorite part?"

"Umm," she started, thinking intently. "They have really great food." She paused. "They have some really great games." Emily appeared stymied and she scrunched her mouth as she searched for something else to say about it.

"Like what?" he asked.

"There's horseshoe tournaments, archery tournaments, baseball, sand volleyball, a fishing derby for the little kids. But there's the usual carnie-type fairway games as well. One of the farmers sets up a petting zoo, and offers donkey rides. There's pie eating contests…"

She peeked at Derrick from the corner of her eye, "Well, the best part is the dance tomorrow night," she said, warming to the subject.

"Your father mentioned something about a dance," Derrick said. "I was hoping you would be willing to dance with me at least once."

She stopped breathing for a second before recovering and answering calmly, "Um, yeah, that would be cool."

"I think your Dad is getting bored, I guess it's time to go back," Derrick said to her, pointing to her father. "I know Katy is really looking forward to seeing you."

"Um, Mr. Nelson," she blurted, and his stomach dropped.

"Please," he interrupted, turning to her. "Call me Caleb," he implored in an effort to deter her, wishing this wouldn't happen.

Her jaw dropped slightly and she breathed in deeply before continuing. "Caleb, I just wanted to tell you that I think you are the best actor in the world. I've seen every single one of your movies a million times."

"Thank you, Emily. It's very kind of you." Did his embarrassment show? He smiled as he internally laughed at himself. "Especially if that includes *One Night of Forever*." He shuddered, purposely cringing in disgust. "What an apt title for that thing. Sitting through it felt like a night of forever."

She giggled, and the sound made him smile. "Ok, I'll admit, I only watched that one three times."

"That's twice more than me," he admitted, laughingly.

They were walking off the bridge, and were nearly back to her dad's truck. "But you've said in an interview that you don't watch your own movies unless you have to, so that doesn't count."

He shook his head. "Ok, you got me. But that one time of watching it was torture."

They were back with her parents and Ted introduced his wife, Jennifer. "Hey, why don't you hop in the back, we'll give you a ride to the house."

Grateful, he jumped on the bumper, and started to climb over the tailgate. His first foot went over easily enough, but his second foot caught at the top, and he fell over, sprawling onto the suitcases inelegantly.

He sat up quickly and waved, letting them know he was all right, and Emily giggled again. Maybe by the end of the weekend, he'd be a mere mortal to her. He could only hope.

****

Katy stood on the porch impatiently waiting for her cousin to arrive with her favorite niece, bouncing from foot to foot, staring down the driveway. At last, the familiar truck rolled into the drive and she couldn't keep herself in check any longer. Barreling out of the house shouting, "Jennifer! Emily! You're here!" at the top of her lungs, she raced down the steps.

Emily didn't wait for the vehicle to come to a complete stop before she threw open her door and jumped out of the cab. Forgetting all dignity, she threw herself into the tight embrace shouting "Aunt Katy!" like a little girl.

They spun around happily and then headed into the house when Derrick's voice sounded from behind them, talking to Ted.

"You want any help hauling these bags?"

Katy's gaze was momentarily diverted behind them, taking in Caleb in all his glory, swallowing the longing and ordering the carbonation to take a night off. It ignored her. "So you met Caleb," she whispered, not even trying to mask the wicked smile and a gleam in her eyes. It had been a long time

66

since she'd been able to gush over boys, and she let herself reverting backward eight years.

Emily sucked air through thin lips and rolled her eyes heavenward. "Oh yeah, I met Caleb." She was flipping her hand in front of her to express the magnitude of that moment.

Katy laughed, almost giggling like a little girl. "He is so... so..."

"Hot?" the teenager supplied. "Incredible? Awesome?"

"Oh, you have *no* idea," she gushed softly, letting her words mimic the gooiness of her inner organs. "He made me *cookies* one night!"

"Out of the way!" Caleb called as he approached them, his arms loaded with Jennifer's suitcase and Emily's duffel bag and pillow. As he slid past, he bumped her hip with his own, nudging her out of the way and gently pushing her into the teenager.

Katy bumped back, and he nearly lost his hold on his cargo. "Watch it, pal!" she called. He spun around with his arms still loaded and flashed them both a wide smile before turning around again and disappearing into the house. She lost her breath for a second and noticed the look of shock on her niece's face.

"What?"

"He has the hots for you, Aunt Katy. He's got it *bad.*"

Did he really? Katy turned that thought over in her mind for a second, considering the possibility. No, Emily was wrong. Several of her temporary boarders over the years had imagined themselves in love with her. A few had even proposed. But it was her home and Tolleson that they really loved, not her. This place got under your skin.

Jerry stuck her head out of the front door. "The pudding is ready!" she hollered. "We've got chocolate or pistachio. Come and get some before Caleb and

Kyle eat it all."

The two of them together walked into the house, headed for the kitchen. As they passed through the living room, Katy reached over the back side of the nearest sofa grabbing a couch pillow and, without breaking stride, changed hands and thwapped Emily over the head with it.

"Oh no, you did *not* just do that!" the teenager exclaimed, running around to the side of the sofa and grabbing one of the thousand pillows scattered around. Snatching the nearest one and hurling it, she clobbered her aunt across the chest. "There! I am the champion pillo—"

Her words were cut off as another pillow slammed into her stomach. Katy took off with a pillow in each hand, running around to the other side of the couch and laughing evilly.

"Oh yeah?" she taunted. "Prove it!"

She lost track of how many projectiles were flying through the room as she dodged, ducked and hurled her own ammunition. The only sound she could hear was the laughter and squealing and the occasional crash or thud.

And then, in one great effort of a final stand, Emily jumped up from behind one of the sofas and hurled her pillow with all her strength. Katy ducked, the pillow flying harmlessly over her head and she whirled around to realize it was headed straight for Caleb, who had just stepped through the kitchen door with a bowl in his hands, his spoon rising to his mouth. With an evil *thud* the pillow hit its mark at full speed, crashing into the bowl, forcing it to lurch backward.

Green and brown pudding splattered all over the man's face and that sexy black shirt, smearing and congealing in his beard and hair. Everyone froze in place, staring at him horrified. His eyes were wide and unfocused, his hand and spoon frozen next to his open mouth, his breath momentarily shocked from him.

And then he pulled his bowl away from his chest and cast his eyes downward with a look of horror. Silence descended for one heartbeat before he wailed "My pudding!" His eyes lifted and narrowed, looking around the room to identify the culprit.

"The wasting of pudding is a very serious offence," he told them. "It is a precious commodity. Who did this?"

Emily, the little brat, couldn't take the pressure and blurted "She started it!" like a five-year-old, pointing at Katy.

"Emily threw the pillow!" Katy hollered, defending her honor and slowly shifting her position to the other side of the couch.

Caleb only shook his head. "I see." With lightning speed, he retrieved the pillow from the floor and sent it hurtling through the living room, smacking Emily in the face, while simultaneously running to the couch toward Katy.

She tried to run, but with surprising grace and agility, he jumped the back and landed on the cushions, still holding his bowl of pudding, and grabbed her before she could escape.

They both tumbled to the ground, Katy laughing and screeching helplessly as he pinned her to the carpet and sat on her hips. The pudding had flown everywhere, covering both of them, but he scooped out what remained into his hand and held it above her face.

"Cry Uncle!" he told her.

"Uncle!" she gasped between her chortles of laughter. "Uncle already!"

He laughed maniacally now with victory as he nailed Emily with one last pillow, licking pudding from his hands, not moving from his position. Katy reached up with a finger and scooped a portion of the green glob off his face and stuck it between her lips, trying to cover her giddiness.

"Mmmm," she said. "Pistachio! Is there any more?"

"I don't know," he admitted and slid off her, holding a hand out to help her up while keeping a wary eye on Emily, in case she had bright ideas of mounting another offensive. "Kyle was making great inroads into the bowl when last I saw."

He smiled at the teenager. "Truce? I'll treat you to a bowl of pudding... and I'll even let you eat it instead of wear it." His tone implied vast amounts of graciousness on his part in this matter.

There he was, standing before her covered in chocolate and pistachio pudding, his hair stuck out at weird angles, his shirt askew, a lopsided smile on his face. He looked kinda...dorky.

Emily shook her head with an amazed smile. "I think I really like Caleb better," she told the man.

Weird.

But what was weirder was Caleb's beaming, chocolate and pistachio smile and wink, followed by a mysterious, "Glad to hear it."

Chapter Seven

Caleb glanced out his bedroom window to the lights shining in the tree house, where all the single women were sleeping that night. It was Katy's night off from work, and they'd decided to have a slumber party—complete with sleeping bags and copious amounts of junk food. Even Elizabeth had braved the rope ladder to participate.

Sighing, his thoughts returned to the problem at hand—the matter of him wussing out. It was the only way he could find to describe why he'd finally made the choice to call for help. Ever since meeting Emily earlier that night, his fantasy bubble had popped. He was delusional to think that he could spend an entire day at a public event and not just go unnoticed, but that *someone* during the day would not ask for an autograph.

The thought made him cringe and feel slightly panicky inside, but he admitted to himself that Katy would have to find out the truth sometime. There was no way he could just walk away from this house now, from *her*, and not look back. This meant, if he wanted any chance at all with her, full disclosure.

He sat on his bed, legs crossed, elbows resting on his knees, and put his cell phone to his ear, holding his forehead in the palm of his free hand. He listened to two rings before the phone was answered.

"What's wrong?" Todd asked immediately, not wasting time with the pleasantries.

"I woke up to reality," Caleb answered reluctantly. "I need low-profile help."

"Are you all right?" the man asked roughly, concerned.

"I'm fine, Todd. I just got myself into a pickle and I'd feel more comfortable with a shadow."

"What's going on?"

"It's a woman," he answered sheepishly, and then he realized he needed to clarify because almost all of his problems were women-related. "I promised her I'd take her to this shindig she wants to go to. So far, I've been keeping a low profile. Only a couple of people know that I'm here, or who I am."

Todd swore under his breath. "You know I'm supposed to check out your dates first," he reprimanded. "This is why Derrick Nelson hadn't been on a real date in over a year and a half. Remember Psycho Fan?"

He shuddered involuntarily. "Yes, Todd. I remember. But it's not like that. Katy doesn't have a clue who I am. And she wouldn't care, either."

Todd snorted disbelievingly.

"Look, just send someone, all right?" Caleb snapped, and then softened. "Someone who can blend into a crowd. Someone who doesn't scream 'bodyguard.'"

His security specialist sighed. "What kind of shindig?"

"Think 'county fair' meets 'community picnic.' I'd like whoever you pick to watch over Katy too, in case someone takes exception to me being with her." He paused. "But I don't want her to know what he is. I'll tell her he's a friend."

"I'm sending five men," Todd informed him.

"I don't need that many," Caleb insisted, watching this outing turn into a PR nightmare of a circus. "Let's not over-react."

"Over-react? Texas, Derrick," his employee reminded. "Remember Texas? How about Albuquerque? Or Phoenix? Ringing any bells here?"

"I'm barely recognizable. I've made it this long, haven't I?"

"Have you gone outside in a crowd yet?" After a short pause, Todd continued, "I didn't think so. Look, I will make sure they are inconspicuous. You'll hardly notice they are there."

"Fine. Whatever," Caleb grumbled reluctantly.

"Where am I sending them, and when do they need to be there?"

He supplied the address of the house and general location of the park where the celebration was being held. "And they've got roughly twelve hours to get there," he added.

If his security specialist was irritated or inconvenienced by the short notice, he didn't let it show in his response. "They'll be there. Just keep an eye out for Eddie, all right?" he advised.

Caleb sighed in relief. He liked Eddie. He'd blend in well.

"And what's Katy's last name?" Todd asked, still all business.

"No, Todd. You will not conduct a background check on her."

"Derrick, be reasonable."

"No!" he shouted. "I moved into Katy's life, not the other way around." He pushed the "end" button before Todd could get in another word, wishing he could slam the receiver into a cradle. The childish action would have gone a long way to relieving some of his pent-up frustration.

But despite his irritation, the gnawing unease in the pit of his stomach had dissipated, and he knew he'd made the right decision. It was safer for all of them this way.

****

Normally Katy would be wearing jeans and a T-shirt. In fact, for the last eighteen years, she'd worn exactly that for this occasion, but today, she was breaking tradition. She was moving beyond her comfort zone and stretching herself as a person, and as a woman. She was wearing a dress. In public.

"Do I look okay?" she asked nervously as she stood in front of her tall mirror, swirling this way and that, letting the yellow fabric billow around her knees.

Jerry and Emily had dressed her, ransacking her closet for the long forgotten pieces of clothing Grandpa had bought her ages ago that had never been used. They'd unearthed a sleeveless yellow cotton summer dress, V necked, cut to the exact same shape as her waist, the hem scalloped into eyelet lace. They'd pulled her hair back into a simple ponytail at the base of her neck, tying a fat, floppy yellow ribbon over the elastic, so that the ends dangled down her back. Emily lent her brown leather sandals.

"You look *hot*," Emily assured her. "He's not going to be able to take his eyes off you!"

Jerry was nodding in agreement. "You're beautiful, Katy."

Katy had to admit, the day was hot, and the dress was light and airy. "All right, if you guys are sure."

"We're sure!" they both said in unison.

"All right, all right," she gave up. "But let's get going. Elizabeth is making Happy Face Pancakes, and I'm starving." She ran from her attic room and barreled down the stairs, excited over breakfast, her favorite meal of the day.

Emily followed her. "You're always starving, Katy." She could almost hear the eye roll in the teenager's tone of voice.

She flounced down the stairs, laughing over her shoulder at her niece, only to turn around and freeze halfway down to the second floor landing. Caleb was at the bottom, staring up at her. His mouth hung slightly open slightly, his eyes intent, scouring her from her hair to her toes. He swallowed and blinked, taking one step up in her direction.

"You are gorgeous," he breathed out.

Everything inside her became fluttery and she lost her footing, tripping slightly, straight into his arms. He caught her easily, but it only made her muscles turn to gooey jelly. Was that him shaking? Or her? It didn't matter, really. If he kept looking at her like that, she'd never be able to use her legs again.

Gently, he set her down and stepped back slightly. "You look like sunshine," he said softly. "That dress is perfect for you."

"Thank you," she said, but it came out so breathlessly, she wasn't sure he could understand her.

He smiled, his eyes still intense. "Today is going to be a very nice day." He kissed her forehead, and grabbed her hand, pulling her to the side so that Jerry and Emily could pass by. "I need to talk to you for a minute if that's all right," he said, his voice becoming nervous.

Uh, oh. This couldn't be good.

****

Now all Caleb had to do was fess up to Katy. He'd been working himself up to it all morning, practicing just the right amount of casualness with the same intensity he reserved for getting into character before shooting. But then she'd walked down those steps, and everything he'd prepared vanished from his mind.

Everything vanished from his mind, and for a moment, he wouldn't have been able to remember his own name. She was exquisite. Everything about her appealed to him. And then she'd fallen into his arms, right where he wanted her anyway.

Jerry coughed, pulling him from his stupor, and

he remembered he had a mission in seeking Katy out this morning. Time to fess up.

She stood in front of him looking up expectantly. She was reading his body language, and he could tell she knew he was nervous. He breathed in deeply, gathering his courage.

"Remember that I told you I was an actor?" he asked, building up to his admission. She nodded, waiting patiently. "Well, I've played in a few movies," he told her. "There's a small chance someone might recognize me today, and ask for an autograph." He paused, studying her face, waiting for a reaction. But the best he could guess was a "Huh. Really?" look. "I just wanted to let you know ahead of time, so things wouldn't get weird, in the off chance that happens."

"So people stop you and ask you for your autograph?" she asked, processing this information in her mind.

"Sometimes," he said, in what had to be the largest understatement of the century. He was so guilty of underplaying the truth, he was bordering on outright lying. But now was not the time to say "Yeah, one time I was assaulted by a crowd of crazed fans when they managed to separate me from my bodyguard." There wasn't a single part of his body that had not been grabbed or touched that day. He left that part out, choosing instead to move on to the next confession.

"Another thing." He paused, reluctant to tell her the next part. "I use a screen name. If anyone recognizes me, they'll call me Derrick."

"Derrick?" she asked, incredulous. "Why would you change your name to Derrick? Caleb is such an awesome name!"

He shrugged, remembering his mother's original lamentations that he wouldn't use his first name for his work. "It's my middle name, and I was young.

Derrick sounded more macho to me at the time."

Katy rolled her eyes. "Oh good grief."

He couldn't stop his chuckle from escaping. "And one more thing."

"There's more?" she asked. If only she knew.

"I called a friend last night and invited him to join us today. I hope you don't mind."

She looked relieved. "I don't mind at all, Caleb! Any friend of yours is welcome here." That didn't mean much—*everyone* was welcome in her home.

"He's downstairs being plied with pancakes by Elizabeth."

"Let's go meet him!" she exclaimed happily, grabbing his hand and pulling him to the stairs.

****

Katy skipped into the room, towing Caleb behind her with a death grip on his hand, instantly scanning the room. There was one stranger present—a very large, muscly-type. He had to be taller than Caleb by an inch or two, which would place him over six and a half feet tall. He was wearing cutoff jeans and a T-shirt, and a baseball cap sat on the table next to his breakfast plate. His blond hair would have been neatly combed, if the edges weren't sticking out slightly.

He was shoveling pancakes into his mouth and chatting with Jerry, but when he saw her enter he swallowed quickly and stood up. Overjoyed that Caleb had felt comfortable enough to invite someone, she launched herself at him, enveloping him in a welcome hug.

****

The look of shock and horror on Eddie's face was comical as he tried to put an inch or two of distance between their bodies while patting the woman on the back and casting his eyes at his boss. Caleb nodded his understanding, and the poor man breathed a visible sigh of relief.

The exchange only took a few seconds. Katy jumped back and took his hand in her own, smiling warmly at him. "I am so glad that Caleb invited you!" she exclaimed, sitting down next to his seat, her full attention centered only on him. "So tell me, where are you from? How long are you going to be here? How do you and Caleb know each other, are you an actor too?"

"Uh," he stammered.

Caleb laughed, sitting on the other side of Katy, pulling his chair close to hers and loading his plate. "Honey, you're not giving the man a chance you answer you." And then to Eddie, "She can be overwhelming at first, but she's harmless, honest." His statement had a double meaning which Eddie caught, but Katy stuck her tongue out at him.

"Harmless," she grumbled, forgetting some of her earlier questions, as was Caleb's goal.

"He's only going to be here for the day," he answered the one question he cared about. "He's leaving late this evening."

"Oh no!" Katy declared. "That's not right. The dance isn't going to get over until late. Why not stay here, and leave in the morning?" she asked, casting her eyes pleadingly on the bodyguard.

His eyes darted to his boss. "I, uh…"

"Please?" she asked. "I would worry all night long that you'd get into an accident or something."

Caleb closed his eyes, sighing, his whole body deflating. Turned away from him, she didn't see him nod his head.

"All right, I'll wait until morning," Eddie answered, fighting a smile over how easily his employer was manipulated. "Was that a hotel I saw a few blocks away?"

"Absolutely not," Katy insisted. "No friend of Caleb's is going to stay at a hotel. We have plenty of room." She beamed up at him, her whole body radiating the sunshine that matched the color of her dress.

"It's easier if you don't try to fight her," Jerry advised. "She's going to win in the end."

The woman being discussed only laughed as she finally turned to her plate and her breakfast. "So you still haven't told me how you and Caleb know each other."

But Eddie had recovered his composure, having been given time to think through the earlier asked questions. "We've worked together a few times."

"So you're in movies too?" she asked innocently.

"Um, no, I'm more of a background person."

"What's that like?" she asked with interest. "Caleb doesn't like talking about his work, so I don't ask him. But is it fun?"

Caleb inconspicuously put his arm on the back of Katy's chair, and was thrilled when Katy instinctively leaned slightly closer to him, her attention still on his "friend." Breakfast was a long, slow meal as Eddie was plied with food and conversation and hospitality.

Finally, everyone was stuffed, and it was time to leave for the festivities, but thanks to their hostess, it had felt as if the party had already started.

Chapter Eight

Caleb and Eddie had an odd friendship, Katy decided. They didn't joke around with each other and in fact, they barely even spoke to each other except for the occasional comment here or there. She wondered if his friend was a war veteran suffering from post-traumatic stress disorder. He wouldn't completely relax, and he spent his entire time casually circling the small group of friends, diligently watching the crowd around them, as though he felt something bad was about to happen at any moment. Her heart went out to him, but it was the one dent in an otherwise perfect day.

Perfect, because Caleb was claiming her as his own. And heaven help her, she *liked* it. She liked it that he stood in her personal space. She liked that he held her hand, or put his arm over her shoulders, or around her waist. She liked that he would stand behind her, his arms around her stomach, holding her against his body, and that he would occasionally lean down and nuzzle his face into her hair, breathing in deeply.

"What is that smell?" he asked at last. "It's incredible."

"Orchids," she answered. "I'm trying a new shampoo, since it's my favorite flower."

"I think it's my favorite too," he decided. She'd have to go buy some more, the bottle was almost empty. Anything to keep him this close to her.

So far today the four of them, Katy, Caleb, Jerry and Eddie, watched Harry and George's annual juggling routine, fed the ducks, walked the fairway, played lawn darts, got their faces painted, tried to sink the mayor off his perch into a vast tub of water, threw darts at balloons and participated in the annual watermelon-seed-spitting contest. Jerry won, dethroning a five-time champion. Victor insisted on a re-match, and was told to try again next year.

They watched Ted come in third in the pie-eating contest, much to the embarrassment and humiliation of Emily. They hurried over to the archery contest to be there when Elizabeth took second, and they'd stopped to watch Kyle's mini-concert with his band buddies. They'd taken advantage of the multitude of food vendors, snacking on cotton candy, hot dogs, Indian fry bread, and nachos, drinking countless cups of soda and iced tea.

And now it was time for the game. She'd participated in the annual baseball game against Pecos for the last eight years now, and it had become a bit of a good-natured grudge match with their sister town. Both communities turned up in droves to watch the two teams go head to head. Katy had a score to settle. Pecos had won last year, breaking Tolleson's three year winning streak. She was going to make sure they didn't get two in a row.

She looked up to the bleachers to see the entire household congregated, watching enthusiastically, cheering her on. Jerry put her fingers on either side of her mouth and let out a piercing whistle. Ted, sitting next to a smiling Jennifer, was now wearing his green "Go Katy!" T-shirt that he'd worn for the last five years and shouted encouragement to her. Caleb was standing, clapping and hollering. Elizabeth wore a green "Tolleson" baseball cap, munching on a hot dog and waving a green pennant in her hand.

Kyle was there with his girlfriend and his entire band, Emily sitting with the younger crowd. She'd been with them all day, helping with the concert and flirting with the drummer. They all hollered and clapped, getting into the spirit of the game.

And then there was Eddie. He sat behind Caleb, ostensibly watching the game and cheering as well, but his eyes kept darting around the bleachers, studying the faces and movements of the people around them. Katy sighed. She'd talk to Caleb later. There had to be something she could do for the man.

"You're going *down*, Tolleson!" Sandy Hetherman shouted from her dugout, pulling Katy back to the game.

"In your dreams, Hetherman!" Katy hollered back, repeatedly throwing a baseball into her glove, calming herself with the rhythmic "catch-throw, catch-throw" and loving the sound of the thunk as it connected with the leather. "You don't have a chance!"

She made a mental note that when the game was over she'd have to ask Sandy if her son's new medication was helping him at all, if he was feeling any better. But for now, the woman was a Pecos Girl. There would be no quarter given, no leniency.

Pecos was toast.

****

The sky overhead was a brilliant blue, and surely the birds in the trees were singing. Caleb couldn't be sure, because the crowd around him was yelling and hollering too loudly for him to hear anything over their enthusiasm. Jerry let out a piercing whistle next to him, causing his ears to ring, and he thought about his poor bodyguard, with the expensive communications hardware in his ear.

He leaned back slightly. "You all right?" he asked Eddie, glancing behind him to make sure.

"What?" Eddie asked sarcastically, holding the little device in his hand and rubbing his ear. "I think you might owe me worker's comp after this, Nelson."

Jerry looked embarrassed. "Sorry about that," she said.

"You're going *down*, Tolleson!" some woman on the opposing team hollered loudly, sounding like this was a gang war on the verge of breaking out.

And then, to Caleb's shock and surprise, his kind hearted, loving, generous, "I see the best in everyone" almost/maybe girlfriend hollered back angrily "In your dreams, Hetherman! You don't have a chance!"

He stood there in the stands, staring in shock, but Jerry was laughing so hard that her whole body was shaking. "Fun, isn't it?" she asked.

"Who is that woman, and what did she do with Katy?" Caleb asked as he watched the players warming up.

"She takes her baseball very seriously," Jerry answered.

"Apparently so."

He hadn't noticed that fact before this, he'd been too busy enjoying the sight of Katy in those white stretchy baseball pants and the green T-shirt she'd changed into. Her penny-copper hair rested between her shoulders, held in a ponytail by the adjusting strap of her hat. Who knew a baseball uniform could be so alluring?

"Believe it or not," Jerry told him, "that woman she just yelled at is one of her best friends. They've known each other most of their lives. In fact," she continued, "Katy was a bridesmaid at Sandy's wedding, and even threw her a baby shower a couple of years ago. But see, this is baseball. Not only that, but this is the annual Pecos/Tolleson playoff. There is no such thing as friendship for the next hour and a half. Tomorrow they will be friends again." She paused for a moment. "Well... by the end of the month for sure, at any rate."

"This is a timed game?" Eddie asked behind

them.

"It won't go over that time, because of the dance. But they'll go a full nine innings if they play fast enough."

Both teams lined up on either side of the field as a little girl stepped onto the infield. She cleared her throat and music started playing through a loudspeaker. The players removed their hats, and the crowd stood at attention as the national anthem was sung.

Then Tolleson won the coin toss and chose to field first. Katy was on the pitcher's mound, watching as the batter stepped up to the plate. Her eyes were intense and calculating. Leaning forward, she pulled the ball behind her back, prepping for the windup. She was totally and completely focused.

Caleb fell onto the bleachers, the wind knocked out of him as he stared at her, watching her every movement. One of his hands reached up to his face, rubbing over his mouth. It was then that he knew he was not a normal man. Other men loved lingerie commercials and scantily clad women. But him, all he needed to get worked up was Katy in a baseball uniform, winding up to pitch, chewing on a wad of bubble gum. How on earth could baseball be so *sexy*? Her knee rose with her glove and her arm, and she let loose. The ball slammed into the catcher's mitt, nearly knocking the player backward.

"Strike!" the umpire yelled.

Caleb was instantly back on his feet, yelling and screaming with the rest of the Tolleson crowd, stomping his feet and clapping. Jerry whistled again encouragingly.

The catcher threw the ball back to the pitcher's mound and Katy caught it effortlessly, tossing it into her glove several times while blowing bubbles with her gum and scraping the dirt with the toe of her cleats. She studied the catcher intensely, shaking her head a couple of times until her teammate made a signal she liked. Winding up, she let loose and a perfect sinker flew over the plate as the batter swung away.

"Strike two!" the umpire yelled.

The crowd went wild. You'd think it was the bottom of the ninth inning of a tied World Series. She continued to fire away her pitches—three batters up, three batters down. Caleb admitted to himself that the other night, when she had casually mentioned her grandfather had taught her how to throw a curve ball, the statement obviously did not express her skill level. She was incredible.

And then he learned that watching her bat was almost as much fun as watching her pitch. She looked cute in the helmet, and there was a fluid gracefulness in the way that she pulled the bat back, her knees slightly bent.

"She's not a strong batter," Jerry informed them. "It bugs her."

But she connected with the ball and was able to get to first base and runner on second and third without getting tagged out. He whistled and stomped and hollered "Atta girl!" feeling pride in her ability.

The next batter, he was told, was their best hitter. The outfielders backed up slightly, the base runners leading off. He held his breath. The first pitch was a ball. The second one a strike. But the third connected, flying high in the air. Across the sky it traveled, and all the runners sprinted around the bases, their arms pumping, holding nothing back.

The ball didn't quit make it over the fence, hitting the ground and almost instantly retrieved by the able fielder. Katy was rounding third base, headed home and she was running to beat the ball which was now on a collision course to tag her out.

Falling backward, she slid the last several feet, kicking the dirt into a cloud that obscured all visibility.

The umpire was standing behind the mayhem and as the cloud dissipated he threw his hands wide and flat. "Safe!" he hollered.

Caleb screamed some more, stomping and clapping with the rest of the crowd.

The rest of the game was just as nerve-wracking. By the end of the sixth inning, they were tied, five to five. Katy had thrown her body in front of the ball more times than Caleb wanted to see, and had almost been kicked off the field once for yelling at the umpire.

The score remained gridlocked for the next four innings, although it was close several times. Katy struck out once, and Caleb could only laugh at the invective that burst from her mouth. She was warned by the umpire and she stomped off to the dugout in disgust over her batting.

Thirty minutes later, the game was running fifteen minutes late, in the top of the twelfth inning and now tied six to six. The umpires tried to call the game, but the crowd nearly rioted, so in fear for their life, they let it continue.

Pecos managed to gain one run before earning their third out. Tolleson's first batter struck out, but their second batter was able to hit a single. Katy stepped up to the batter's box, and Caleb's stomach jumped into his throat. She wasn't their strongest hitter, and if she struck out, she'd be heartbroken. Or spitting mad. He wasn't sure which.

The first pitch was a strike.

Suddenly, the runner on first base took off, stealing to second, and there was a moment of panic as the opposing catcher hurled the ball to the base. The screaming crowd drowned out the umpire's voice, and Caleb only knew she was safe by his hand gestures.

The second pitch was a ball.

The count filled; Katy was at two and three. The next one was the do-or-die pitch. He held his breath and chanted over and over again, "You can do this you can do this you can do this!"

Her bat connected and the ball shot through the infield, one foot above the ground at shin level. Infielders dove, but the ball was too fast and just barely out of reach of their gloves as it hurtled into the outfield. Katy sprinted to first and then to second as a runner dove home, tying the game once again.

Then their strongest hitter stepped up, bat held high, her face glaring at the pitcher. It only took one pitch; she swung and the ball was gone to the back fence. Katy ran to third, and then, amidst the screaming of two towns, without breaking stride, she headed for home and scored the final run.

The game finally ended after two hours and twelve innings with a score of nine to seven, in Tolleson's favor. Caleb couldn't remember ever watching a World Series that had been as exciting, nerve wracking, and satisfying. Everyone in the stands was jumping up and down and hugging each other. His voice was hoarse with all the shouting he'd done, but he couldn't care. His girl had won, and scored the winning run.

Chapter Nine

As Emily had said earlier, Caleb looked *hot* tonight, Katy mused. His hair was combed back off his face, his beard was neatly trimmed and shaped and those large obnoxious sunglasses which had been hiding his face all day were finally gone. He was wearing a chocolate brown button-down shirt that matched his eyes exactly. The top two buttons were undone, and a thin black tie was knotted in the middle of chest. And those black jeans... well... Katy had to remind herself to breathe just remembering how well they shaped his thighs and backside.

Luckily, she didn't have to rely on memory. All she had to do was raise her eyes to the dance floor to see him sliding by gracefully with Elizabeth in his arms. His attention was fixed on his dance partner, and something the older woman said made him laugh merrily, his eyes twinkling. He responded and it was her turn to laugh.

He was, by far, the most handsome man in attendance, and Katy knew she wasn't the only one to think so. Half the women at the dance were staring at him longingly. They'd received numerous curious stares as they walked onto the converted ball field, where her team had been victorious and where the dance was being held.

He was also a perfect gentleman. The very first song after arriving, he asked if Emily would give him the honor and Ted, camera mysteriously ready, snapped enough pictures to fill half his memory chip. Caleb allowed several serious photos to be taken before getting bored. He dipped the teenager, gave her bunny ears, and told her to jump into his arms so that he was holding her bridal style. By the time the song was over, they were collapsing with laughter and could barely stumble back to the table, all documented by her cousin.

Then it was Katy's turn. The band was playing a slow, schmaltzy song and he pulled her into his arms, holding her close. She was eternally grateful at that moment that Grandpa had insisted on teaching her how to dance, because Caleb molded their bodies together as he slowly led her across the grass, every nuance, every breath indicating which direction he wanted to go, where he wanted to turn. The sway and movement was lulling and intoxicating at the same time.

Her head only reached his shoulder and she rested there, feeling his breath on her ear when he leaned over and kissed her temple, his steps never faltering. "Katy," he whispered with a soft, sad voice. "I think I'm starting to fall in love with you." He tightened the arm around her waist, pulling her closer as if he were afraid she'd run away from him.

She lost her footing, tripping them up slightly. But he had such a good hold on her that they didn't fall over. The Jolt rush didn't even begin to describe what was happening inside her at that moment. "You can't tell a girl that, and expect her stay on step," she reprimanded weakly and he chuckled into her hair. "Especially when she's feeling the exact same way," she told him softly.

Another rush of air glided over her ear. "Good," he whispered.

They didn't talk again, letting the rhythm of the music communicate with the sway of their bodies as they glided over the dance floor, telling each other everything they needed to know at that moment. She closed her eyes, choosing to just feel his arms around her, his body against her, the synchronicity of their legs moving in harmony.

Right now, at this moment, she could believe in magic.

All too soon the song ended, and he held her hand as he led her back to their table, squeezing gently as she lowered herself into her seat. He kissed her cheek, and then turned to Elizabeth, throwing his head back slightly and plastering his charming smile across his face.

"Lizzy," he said, "will you dance with me?" He held his hand out to her pleadingly.

"I don't know," she hedged, casting a glance at Katy. "You are too young and energetic for me. You almost gave me a heart attack the other night."

"Hogwash," he said. "You can dance circles around me and you know it."

Katy nodded encouragingly, and Elizabeth sighed deeply. "All right," she relented, as though he had asked for a kidney instead of a dance. "If you're forcing me..." But the twinkle in her eye gave lie to her words and there was a skip in her step as the two moved to the edge of the crowd.

The music was upbeat, and Caleb instantly jumped into a swing routine that Elizabeth followed easily and energetically with childish delight. He had made her entire night, and Katy felt all mushy and gooey inside watching him make their elderly roommate so happy. The wonderful thing about him was that he did it so effortlessly, so thoughtlessly. He wasn't *trying* to be nice. He just simply *was*.

Another duo passed by, and Katy watched Jerry and Eddie dancing in the same vicinity as Caleb and Elizabeth. They were talking easily enough, smiling and getting along wonderfully. But the man's attention wasn't focused on his partner; he was watching his friend and the couples around them.

She sighed, sad for him and sad for her friend

who was probably feeling slighted. Jerry didn't look like it, though. In fact, she looked completely comfortable, and like she was having a fantastic time.

When the song ended, all four of them started back for the table. As they drew closer, one of the teenagers from the Pecos baseball team approached from a nearby table, her eyes intent on Caleb. They all arrived at the same time, and the young woman shifted nervously from one foot to the other before shoving out a hand holding a napkin and a pen.

"I'm sorry, Mr. Nelson, I didn't want to disturb you while you were dancing, but I was hoping I could get an autograph?" She bit her lip, her eyes scared.

He smiled kindly at her, and Katy knew that the girl wouldn't be able to detect the slight stiffening of his body. "Sure," he answered the girl, taking the proffered items. "What's your name?"

"Heather," she told him.

Eddie casually stepped up behind Caleb, closing the distance between them. "That was a great game you played today," he said conversationally to the girl as he signed the napkin, ignoring the proximity of his friend. "You are an excellent third baseman."

Her eyes were wide, her mouth hanging open slightly. "Th... thank you," she stammered. Now she was completely besotted, and Katy could wholly understand how the poor girl was feeling. Caleb apparently had the same effect on many women. The teenager cast her eyes on the napkin and choked. "Thank you!" she expressed again, and stumbled away, back to her table across the field.

"What did you put on that napkin?" Katy asked laughingly.

He shrugged, obviously thinking it wasn't a big deal. "The exact same thing I told her."

"It might be time to leave," Eddie said abruptly behind Caleb.

"Not yet," he grumbled, holding his hand out to Katy again. "May I have this dance?" he asked, as if there was the possibility she'd say no.

On the way out to the dance floor they were stopped by another teenager with a pen and napkin, and once again he smiled kindly and signed Derrick Nelson. Eddie, who was dragging Jerry with him to the dance floor again, grumbled under his breath, but Caleb ignored him.

He pulled her into his arms and started dancing, pursing his lips slightly. "I'm afraid Eddie is right," he told her reluctantly. "I'm going to have to leave the dance soon."

Disappointment gripped her heart, but she tried not to let it show. She wasn't successful, because he sighed, looking in her eyes. "I don't want to."

"It's only a couple girls," she argued, wondering what his problem was.

He breathed heavily, looking for a way to explain it to her. "Right now, yes, it's just a couple of girls, but—"

"Katy! Caleb!" Emily interrupted them, gasping for breath as she crashed into them, unable to stop in time from her momentum. "You have to get out of here, *now.*"

Instantly, Eddie was beside them, and four other men that looked vaguely familiar suddenly appeared around them, creating a circle. Caleb pulled her closer, his grip tightening as his heart raced.

"Who are these men?" she asked, starting to feel slightly claustrophobic, and wondering why Caleb seemed to already know them. Had these strangers been *following* them all day?

"What's going on?" Eddie asked the teenager, ignoring her.

"It's that Meghan Stirlidge," Emily spat the name disgustedly. "I heard her talking to her friends. They've all figured out about Derrick, and they're texting every friend they have in the county. You have roughly fifteen minutes before all hell breaks loose."

"These men are here to protect us," Caleb whispered softly in Katy's ear. "I'll explain later."

Katy looked over to the table where Elizabeth was guarding her purse and saw a small crowd of girls waiting for their return. She glared at Caleb suspiciously as a weird feeling started to take over. "How many movies have you been in?"

"Several," he replied tersely, his arms a steel band around her.

"We need to get you out of here," Eddie said brusquely.

Caleb sighed deeply. "We still have a few minutes," he said. "Katy's friends are being very civilized, and we have to pass by them anyway to get to the car. I'm going to sign a few autographs for them on the way out."

Eddie scowled. "That's cutting it close. Todd's going to be mad."

"Let Todd get mad," he returned. Then he looked down at Katy, still held tightly in his arms. "I'm so sorry about this, honey. I was hoping it wouldn't end this way. You don't need to leave if you don't want to; the circus will end once I go."

She shook her head. "Don't think you're getting out of it that easily, buster," she declared sternly. "You have questions to answer."

For the first time since the fiasco started, a small smile broke over his face, lighting his eyes and he stifled a chuckle. "All right then. In that case, whatever happens, don't let go of me. Hold on however you have to."

Holy crow, what was he expecting? For these girls to mob him senselessly? It was like he was a quarterback making a game plan in a huddle.

"In the event we do get separated, hold on to one of these gentlemen here, they'll get you out."

She looked around at the new faces, trying to memorize them. They all looked very serious, and very tough looking. She smiled weakly, waving slightly. Some of them softened slightly, hiding smiles or nodding while staying focused.

"You ready?" Caleb asked her. Personally, she didn't see the big deal, but she nodded, trying to hide a giggle. "All right, let's do this."

Keeping her glued to his side, he headed for the growing crowd of women with a bright smile on his face. He raised his hand in a small wave and camera flashes illuminated the ball field almost as effectively as the park lights. "Smile, darlin'," he whispered to her. "The world is about to meet you."

It had to be the actor in him, he was so melodramatic.

The mysterious men reorganized around them, Eddie in the front looking suspiciously official and commanding, two on either side of them. Somewhere along the way, Jerry had disappeared, probably getting out while the getting was good.

As they drew nearer to the crowd, excited voices rose, growing louder and louder. Katy couldn't help it, she was feeling impish. She leaned up as far as she could with his arm gripping her around the waist and teased, "'Someone *might* recognize me,'" she quoted ruthlessly. "'I don't want things to get *weird* if that should happen.'"

He laughed, causing even more flashes to explode around them as he hugged her tighter to his side. "Just shut up, all right?"

"'They *sometimes* ask me for an autograph,'" she continued.

"You're not going to let me live this down, are you?"

"Not for a very, very long time."

And then his mouth was at her ear for a second, taking her by surprise and causing her stomach to replace her heart. "That sounds really, really good to me," he told her, before he stood erect and accepted the first item being handed to him and smiling at the lucky young woman.

The bodyguards had locked wrists with each other, creating a human barricade and keeping the masses a few feet away. They made slow progress, inching to the exit gate, women calling to "Derrick Nelson," professing undying love and adoration of his acting ability and paying homage to his breathtaking looks.

He had to let go of Katy to sign the napkins and cups and paper plates being shoved in his face, and he did his best to scrawl his name across each as quickly as he could, asking for names and smiling at the owners, handing their items back over the arms of his human shield. She followed his earlier instructions and kept a vise grip on his waist, smiling at the crowd, proud of what a good sport he was being when he was so disappointed over the abrupt end to the evening.

The crowd grew in size, becoming more rowdy, and Katy realized that she recognized fewer and fewer faces. They became louder and started crushing in on them, actually pushing on the barricade. One woman tried to duck under the connected arms, but Eddie grabbed her before she was able to jump on Caleb, and hauled her off to the side, literally tossing her out of the way.

Katy gulped. The fun suddenly gone, and she began to shake.

"Are your friends gone?" Caleb asked her and she nodded.

"I don't know these people."

His arms wrapped around her again, holding her tightly and comforting her. "All right, Eddie, get us out of here." He ducked his head and closed in on himself, drawing her in with him.

Immediately the men closed in tighter, picking up the pace as they continued to the parking lot. They were now surrounded by a sea of hundreds of screaming women, clawing and grasping, trying to touch the man Katy adored. She wanted to rip their arms off.

He was hers.

He had been *nice* to them, and this is how they thanked him? She was so furious she was shaking and if Caleb hadn't been gripping her so tightly she'd have lashed out on the nearest screaming woman. He must have thought she was scared because he put a hand over her head, pulling her in close to his chest.

"It's all right," he soothed. "It's almost over. They won't let anything happen."

Little did he know that right now, his bodyguards were protecting several of these adolescent twerps from *her*. She couldn't remember being this angry in her entire life. This far exceeded anything she'd ever experienced, and the adrenaline pumped through her blood, begging for relief.

She clamped her jaw shut and followed the flow of the men around her until finally they arrived at a black van, the side door held open by Ted with Jennifer in the driver's seat. "We enlisted some help," Eddie explained over his shoulder as Caleb and Katy were lifted inside. He and two of the men followed, still strategically surrounding them.

The door slammed and the noise level instantly muffled slightly. The engine started and the van began to inch forward.

Eddie scowled. "You like to push your luck, don't you, Nelson?"

Their progress was hindered by the mob surrounding them. "Run over them!" Katy exclaimed and Caleb's face spun around, shocked and laughing.

"You have to play nice, Katy," he informed her. "It's because of them that I have a job." He paused for a second, still smiling. "That went rather well, I thought."

His lead bodyguard considered that for a second. "Yeah, it could have been worse. But if we don't get out of here soon, some of those outlying towns will get a chance to arrive."

"I'm workin' on it!" Jennifer grumbled.

"Run over them!" Katy repeated, wishing she could push her sister-in-law out of the driver's position and do the job herself.

A loud *BANG* pounded against the van and Katy shot from her seat headed for the door, but Caleb grabbed her shirt, halting her progress, and then got his hands around her waist and pulled her back, pushing her down on the seat next to him. He put his arm around her, keeping her pinned to his side.

"No, Katy," he laughed. "You can't take them all on."

"Let me try," she insisted, feeling invincible. She could claw their eyes out easily enough. Later, she would be shocked at herself but for now, she was protecting her man.

Caleb was still laughing at her and hugged her from the side. "I prefer to have you here with me," he told her between his chuckles.

Police sirens cut through the noise, parting the crowd around them. Four cruisers pulled into the parking lot, forcing the multitude to disperse slightly as the black and white vehicles positioned themselves around the van.

"You called in the cavalry, huh?" Caleb asked, looking out the windows.

"I thought it prudent," Eddie answered.

"Good call, man. You've done well tonight. I'll let Todd know, you deserve a raise for that fiasco."

Margie L. Miller

A corner of Eddie's mouth lifted ruefully, and
Katy wondered why. "Thank you," was all the
bodyguard said in that regard. "They were pretty...
irritated... that we didn't give them advance
warning of your appearance, though. We didn't make
any friends in this matter."

"I'll make a donation to their precinct to express
my apologies," Caleb said, sighing. "It wasn't
supposed to be an 'appearance.' It was supposed to
be a nice evening out with my girlfriend, celebrating
her victory."

His girlfriend. Luckily he was looking out the
front window, so he missed her unguarded moment
of pleasure at hearing those words.

The police escorted them from the parking lot at
a snail's pace, and none of the pedestrians were
injured in the process, much to Katy's chagrin.
Where had this intolerant, bloodthirsty side come
from? It usually reserved itself for baseball.

"We can't go back to Gilfrey's," Caleb said.
"Everyone knows where Katy lives, her place will be
mobbed."

"My friends won't go there," she told him. "And I
don't know any of those nutjobs out there. But it
looks like they are going to follow us home."

"Don't worry, I can lose them," Jennifer said
with determination as she wove their van through
the crowded parking lot.

Finally they were on open road, past the mobs
and the dangerously-parked vehicles, and Jennifer
was able to put her foot to the gas pedal. Katy sighed
and settled back into her seat beside Caleb, initially
cuddling into the crook of his arm. The fifteen-
minute trip home lasted over an hour as her sister-
in-law drove a circuitous route through farmlands
and irrigation roads used only by the most local of
locals. In the middle of Stedman's Farm, they even
switched vehicles.

Curiosity emerged within Katy, then turned to resolution. Her good humor began to abate, and when they loaded into the new van, she chose to sit on the opposite side of the bench seat from her "boyfriend." The longer she sat in silence thinking about Caleb's notoriety, the more her stomach burned. All this time, he'd lived under their roof, letting them think he was a penniless vagrant waiting for a big break. He must have had a good laugh every night.

Embarrassment curled its way around her heart, causing it to race and flaming her face. He was famous. Girls literally threw themselves at him. He'd seen in her in her pajamas and bunny slippers. He'd seen her in the morning with pillow lines across her face. She constantly pigged out in front of him, just to get him to eat more, and he didn't even need her to!

Was she some kind of joke? Was he bored? Why on earth would he *do* that to her and her family? She was just like every other woman on that field tonight, with the crush and the twitter-patted heart. The only difference was that they had seen him at work, and she had never had that pleasure.

That realization took root and grew. If she was going to join the throng of his admirers, she should fulfill the part completely. His moratorium on discussing his job was officially over.

When at last they pulled into the familiar circular driveway, Jennifer cut off the engine and everyone looked at the house in silence for a moment.

"I want to see a Derrick Nelson film," Katy declared firmly, leaving no room for questions or debate. *"Right now."*

Chapter Ten

Caleb's heart sank to his stomach. He didn't want to sit around watching one of his old movies tonight. Now that things had calmed down and there was no one to project her fury on, Katy was at a low simmer. Watching a movie would just delay the inevitable.

He had questions to answer and as much as he didn't want to answer those questions, the longer the conversation was ignored, the bigger the wall between them would grow. It had hurt when she pulled away from him in the van, and the ice emanating from her chilled him.

Somehow, despite his best efforts, he had managed to sabotage this relationship before it even had a chance.

"You said I had questions to answer. Don't you think you should ask them?"

She leveled hard eyes on him, keeping her cold anger contained. "Are you sure you want to have that conversation now?" she asked.

It was a warning, and the other occupants of the vehicle heard it as well, escaping as quickly as they could.

But Caleb nodded, clenching his jaw. "We need to talk."

"Fine," she said brusquely. "Let's talk."

Katy pushed herself out of the SUV and stalked away, leaving Caleb to scramble after her. She made her way around the side of the house until she was in the backyard, and then headed for the massive tree, climbing the rope ladder to the house in its branches. He vaguely noted that Eddie was following them at a discreet out-of-hearing distance as he started his own ascent.

As he stepped into the structure, he saw her pacing with restless energy, her hands on her hips. Leaning back against the wall behind him next to the door, he put his hands in his pockets and waited for the storm. But again, she surprised him.

Instead of unleashing her fury, she stopped her pacing and seemed to fold in on herself, dropping onto a small stool across the room. She leaned forward, placing her elbows on her knees and lowered her head, so that all her beautiful hair fell into a curtain, blocking off any view he had of her face.

"Why did you lie to me?" she asked with a wobbly voice. "Why didn't you tell me the truth?"

She was trying not to cry, and Caleb felt completely helpless. He could handle anger. If she was yelling at him right now, he'd be fine. But her misery was out of his depth and he felt like he was drowning.

He could tell her that he technically never lied. But he knew he hadn't been completely forthcoming either. That was really what she was asking. She felt deceived.

"I was only supposed to be here for one night," he started softly. "I didn't know..." he paused, searching for the right words but his mind was blank. "I just didn't know," he repeated.

He didn't know that in such a short time, she'd completely bewitch him, and he didn't know how on earth he was going to reconcile the huge gap between his notoriety and the life she'd built for herself here. So he had closed his eyes and pretended he could be with her, that everything was normal—that *he* was normal.

Sliding downward until he was on the floor, he bent his knees upward and folded his arms over his stomach. He closed his eyes and leaned his head against the wall. "You were so incredible." He paused, trying to find the right words. "And you saw *me*, and I wanted you to keep seeing *me*." He opened his eyes again, staring at her hair and willing her to look at him. "When I realized I couldn't leave you, I knew I'd have to tell you the truth, but I didn't know how."

"'I have to have five bodyguards follow me around' would have been a good start," she told him acidly, finally raising her eyes to glare at him.

"I didn't want to ruin the day," he said weakly, and she scoffed. "Look, I'm sorry," he pleaded. "More sorry than you will ever know."

Caleb covered his face with his hands, terrified she was going to ask him to leave now. There was a long silence drawing out his agony before he heard her intake of breath.

"I feel like the brunt of a horrible joke, Caleb."

"There was nothing funny about any of this at any time," he said, desperately trying to get her to understand. "You are so different from all of them. I couldn't walk away. I didn't want to."

He waited for an agonizingly long moment.

"Is there anything else you've neglected to tell me?" she asked at last.

He dropped his hands from his face and looked up at her hesitantly. She was studying the wall above his left shoulder intently. "I'm worth forty five million dollars and I don't sleep with pajamas on," he said.

"Forty five million," she breathed out with a slightly panicky look.

"I think so. My accountant keeps sending me financial statements trying to tell me how he's investing my money, but I haven't looked at them recently."

She choked slightly, paused, and then out of nowhere declared, "I could have gotten cherries, too."

His bark of laughter startled her, and a thin smile emerged on her face. He breathed a few times, trying to stop the hope from rising in his chest.

"Do you want me to leave?" he whispered at last, all humor gone as stared at the floor.

He heard her rise from the stool and her footsteps grow closer as she approached him. She knelt between his knees and placed her hands on either side of his face, guiding it upward so that his eyes met hers.

"No." She shook her head. "I don't want you to leave."

He wrapped his arms around her waist and pulled her in close to his body, burying his face into her neck, breathing in her smell.

"I'm still mad at you," she told him severely.

"That's okay," he said. "I'm okay with you being mad at me. Just don't tell me you never want to see me again."

"No, I'm not saying that," she said against his chest.

He thought he could hear a "For now" in her tone of voice, and it scared him. Nothing had been resolved, but it seemed that she was willing to begin to forgive his deception. Eventually, though, their lives would have to diverge again. The thought planted an ache in his chest; he still couldn't find a way to reconcile their lifestyles. He couldn't ask her to spend her life under a microscope, having to be suspicious of everyone she met.

"But I am telling you that I am going into the house and watching a Derrick Nelson movie right now."

He groaned. "Do you *have* to?"

"No, I don't have to. But I want to, so I am going

to."

"I really, really, really wish you wouldn't."

She pulled back, putting a hand on his chest to brace herself. "I want to see what all the fuss is about."

"It won't help," he told her seriously. "I see my face every morning in the mirror, and I was there for all the movies. After three years, I still can't figure out what all the fuss is about."

"Three years?" she asked, looking at him curiously.

"I've been acting since the age of eleven, and I started in independent movies when I was seventeen," he explained, drawing out the story longer than he needed to. "Four years ago I landed a leading role in one of those low budget independent films. For some inexplicable reason, it broke box-office records with its ticket sales, and then broke more records with its DVD sales. Like what happened with *The Blair Witch Project* and *Napoleon Dynamite*. Only worse."

He pursed his lips before adding "Honestly, I think they fell in love with the character I played, and the fans transferred that affection to me. It's all I can figure."

Katy rolled her eyes. "Oh yeah, *that* was it," she said as she started to climb out of his embrace. "That's the one I want to see now."

He tightened his hold, stopping her escape, and pulled her against his chest again. "Am I forgiven?" he asked softly.

"Some," she said.

"How about if I let you get cherries in your chocolate malt on Monday?"

She paused briefly. "A little more. But I feel like I am accepting a bribe."

"Whatever works," he whispered, and lowered his face to hers, letting their lips touch ever so lightly.

She gasped, but didn't pull away, speaking against the feather-soft pressure of his mouth. "You're just trying to keep me from watching that movie," she accused helplessly.

"No," he denied quietly. "I wouldn't stoop so low."

He put his hand behind her head, pulling her closer, letting their mouths completely meld together for a single moment as he tasted her. A low electric current started in his fingertips and ran upward through his arms, his chest and stomach, and then into his legs and out his feet. It was a sensation he'd never experienced before, and he gasped, laying his forehead against hers for support.

He couldn't open his eyes, but he felt her nose slide against his briefly, intensifying the current. She was breathing heavily, and he was gratified that he wasn't the only one having difficulty.

"Wow," she said between gasps.

He nodded against her. "Yeah," he agreed.

Once he was able to gain some control, he opened his eyes to her, ready to kiss her again. But to his chagrin, she pulled away. He was too weak to stop her this time as she successfully backed far enough away that he had to let go.

"Movie time," she announced, sounding like she was recovering from an asthma attack, and headed for the door.

He moaned and fell sideways onto the wooden floor of the tree house.

"Come on, you big baby," she taunted, recovering her composure and already heading down the rope ladder. "Let's go watch some Derrick Nelson."

****

Oh mama, that boy can kiss! Katy thought to herself as she made her way to the house on wobbly legs. Pushing away from him had been one of the hardest things she'd ever done, since she knew he was about to repeat the lovely action. But she needed some clarity, and kissing Caleb only made things more confusing. Because he was more than just Caleb, he was Derrick as well. And she didn't know Derrick at all.

The object of her thoughts caught up to her and slid his hand into hers, intertwining their fingers, causing her heart to beat irregularly again.

"If you're going to insist on this, can I pick the movie?"

"No," she told him, unrelenting. "I want to see the one that made you famous."

"You know, you're so insistent right now but maybe it's not available," he realized, sounding hopeful. "It's late at night. You don't have a twenty-four hour DVD rental place around here, do you?"

They were in the house, and Jerry was in the kitchen popping popcorn. "What movie are you looking for?" she asked, unconcerned with the glare that Caleb pierced her with.

"The movie that made Caleb famous," Katy answered her.

Their roommate reached over a counter to a stack of DVD's and sorted through them, picking one from the middle of the pile. "Here you go," she supplied helpfully. "*Cold Fire.*"

The case was tossed onto the table beside them.

"Thank you, Jerry," Caleb said sarcastically.

"No problem," she smiled at them, pulling her bag of popcorn from the microwave and shaking it. Ripping it open and pouring the contents into a large bowl, she held it out to them, offering a bite. "Jennifer told me that Cary Grant was usurped by Derrick Nelson tonight. I came prepared."

"You don't have to stick around for this, you know," Katy informed him, irritated and wondering why he was so adamant about keeping this from her.

What other secrets was he hiding?

"But you'd prefer it if I stayed," he stated with a grimace. "So I'm staying. I don't even let my family watch my movies when I visit home."

"Why are you so dead set against watching yourself on screen?"

He shuddered. "It's embarrassing. I see every mistake I made throughout the whole thing. I keep thinking 'Ugh, I should have done this differently' and 'Wow, that was weak.'"

"Well, keep your comments to yourself, then," she decided, picking up the DVD case and moving into the living room, towing him behind her. "I want to experience this at its full potential. I can get the commentary the next time."

He cringed.

She realized that the only person missing from the household was Kyle, no doubt partying with his band buddies. He probably wouldn't return this evening. Even Eddie was sitting on a corner of a couch, avoiding Caleb's eyes. Jerry sat next to him, propping the bowl of popcorn between them on their connected thighs.

Surrounded by friends and family, she fell onto the couch, snuggling into Caleb as the movie was put in the player and the lights dimmed. The opening credits started rolling, and everyone cheered when Derrick Nelson appeared. He groaned, and she thwapped his stomach.

"Don't ruin my fun," she warned, and he made a zipping motion across his mouth.

The movie began in heaven, and her breath was knocked out of her with the first shot of Caleb. He was a spirit, waiting to be born, and he was dressed in a white so pure, it was nearly blinding. His hair was a silvery crystal color that reflected light, splitting it into countless colors. His eyes were a brilliant, piercing blue.

He looked so different that within the first ten minutes of the movie, she stopped making comparisons. Damon was an entity of his own; his mannerisms, his speech patterns, the lilt of his voice, his very laugh was completely foreign.

Her heart broke when, shortly before Damon's turn to be born onto earth arrived, Satan seduced him away from heaven. The angel fell, forfeiting his right to a body, and everything about him changed. His hair became a brownish, reddish black color, his eyes turned to red orbs, without irises. The shining glory that emanated from him disappeared, replaced with a constant dark shadow.

He became the epitome of evil, hating every human with a consuming obsession because he would never experience what it was to breathe, to taste, to touch, to *feel* with a physical body. He quickly became Satan's best demon, tempting and seducing countless humans to their eternal damnations, finding glory in their misery. He was cold and terrifying, and more than once she cringed into Caleb's side with fear.

But one day, Damon saw a woman that changed everything and the impossible happened—the demon fell in love. He began to defy Satan's orders, protecting the woman, watching over her, fighting off the other demons. As the movie progressed, he was forced to face the consequences of his actions in the lives he'd helped to destroy through the centuries.

And then, when Damon was alone, surrounded by an army of demons intent on destroying his beloved Ghiana, he cried out to God to do what he could not do—protect the woman so that she could return to heaven and be with her husband. As the agonized words left his mouth, a white pillar of light descended, surrounding her, then lifted into the sky.

She was gone, taken back to their creator.

Damon's eyes followed the ascension of the light as it lifted into the sky and for the first time in thousands of years, he smiled.

The credits started rolling.

"What!" Katy screamed, jumping up and leaning forward to the screen. "That was the end?"

"Yes," Caleb told her calmly.

"Is there an alternate ending somewhere? An extended version?"

He shook his head. "No, there isn't."

She grabbed a pillow and threw it at the screen, hollering while the family laughed at her.

"I told you not to watch it," he reminded her calmly.

She turned glaring eyes at him. "Shut up."

He didn't ask her how his acting was, or if she liked the movie. But she now definitely understood why so many women sacrificed dignity and honor for the chance of seeing him in the living flesh.

His character had been breathtaking. When he was an angel, he was light and love and goodness and hope and everything wonderful in the universe. When he was evil he was dark and unconflicted, malicious and cold. But he did it with style, always looking drool-worthy—probably why he was so successful as a demon. And then when he became something in between, locked between the choices he'd already made and the choices he wanted to make, she found herself praying on his behalf for redemption.

But Damon was not Caleb. Never once had the angel/demon done anything that made her think, "Oh, that is *so* Caleb".

"Don't worry, Aunt Katy, we all had the same response," Emily told her.

"So you've seen a Derrick Nelson movie now," he said. "Is your curiosity satisfied?"

She shook her head. "Not in the slightest." He

moaned, falling back into the cushions.

Katy heard various "goodnight's" being said and realized the room was emptying. Quickly, they were alone. He was still lying back on the couch.

"You were wrong earlier," she told him, turning on the seat so that she was facing him, one leg bent onto the cushions in front of her, the other draped over the front. "I do get it now."

"Let's not talk about my acting, or my looks, all right?" he asked, sitting up. "It's a subject I am thoroughly tired of. When I'm with you, I don't have to *be* anything. At least, I didn't used to."

He sounded sad, like his favorite Christmas present was being returned to the store for a refund against his will.

"I'm not asking you to be anything, Caleb," she told him.

"Nothing will ever be the same again," he lamented sadly.

She realized that her appeal had been her ignorance. And now that was gone. "Are you still interested?" she asked with trepidation.

"Oh honey, you have no idea."

The electric current he'd started with that first kiss in the tree house had never completely disappeared, only dimmed slightly, and now it exploded into full force. He put a hand behind her neck, pulling her close to him. She fell forward onto his chest and his mouth found hers. His breathing was ragged and his kisses, unhurried and intoxicating at first, slowly grew more urgent, more desperate.

"We need to go somewhere more private," he whispered, nibbling her neck and causing all kinds of havoc with her nervous system, shutting down vital organs like her lungs and heart and reducing her spine to gelatin.

But his words washed over her, and she nearly

cried out with the frustration. "No."

He paused, confused because everything about her was screaming "yes." He placed the barest distance between them, looking at her eyes. She was breathing raggedly, desperate to keep control. Her entire body was fighting her.

"I'm so sorry, Caleb," she told him, worried about his reaction. How angry was he going to be? "Getting my degree wasn't the only promise I made my grandfather."

He was tense. He was as turned on as she was. He cared about her. They were consenting adults. In his world, sex wasn't a big deal, and the promise she'd made her grandfather was old fashioned and unheard of. Surely he was thinking that the old man was no longer around to know, and that it didn't matter. But it did matter. A promise was a promise. She felt gauche and embarrassed, prudish and frustrated, because every touch of his had felt so *right*.

He placed his hands on her shoulders, closing his eyes and breathing deeply a few times. "Okay," he said. His voice was strained, but he was trying to hide it. He paused for a second. "Katy, I need you to back up slightly. Please."

Instantly, she placed a couple feet of distance between them so that no parts of their bodies were touching. "I'm so sorry." She'd never let things get this far before. Tears threatened and she swallowed a few times, trying to keep them at bay.

Humiliated, she started to get up and leave but his hand shot out and grabbed her arm, pulling her back down to the couch beside him. "Please don't go," he said.

He didn't try to seduce her, didn't try to talk her into breaking her promise to her grandfather. Instead, he said, "You have more algebra homework due on Monday, don't you?"

What?

"Um, yeah," she admitted, confused.

"Why don't you grab your book and meet me in the kitchen. I'm going to take a very cold shower, and then maybe the two of us can figure out your homework so that you can get another awesome score."

A tear escaped, running down her cheek. He still wanted to be with her, after what she had pulled tonight.

"Please don't cry," he moaned, looking at the ceiling. "I am trying very, very hard to be a gentleman right now."

She sniffled and wiped a tear away. "You are being a perfect gentleman," she assured. "You don't have to help me, though."

"Katy, right now it's the only thing I can think of that will allow me to spend time with you, and still keep everything platonic." He chuckled slightly. "Honestly, can anyone stay aroused while finding the value of z?"

She shrugged. "A person with a math fetish, I guess."

He laughed harder. "Yeah, I guess you're right. But I don't have a math fetish, so it's a safe pastime. And it's also why we'll be at the kitchen table, instead of here on the couch." He got up and kissed her cheek lightly. "Give me fifteen minutes." He paused. "Possibly twenty." And then he disappeared up the stairs to his room.

Katy fell back onto the couch considering a cold shower for herself as well. How could this ever work? He was *famous*. A mob had nearly killed him a couple of hours ago, and it was "business as usual." He could have his pick of any woman on the planet, while she was a summer distraction between gigs. Eventually he would wake up and get bored.

But what if he didn't? What if they continued to

spend time together? Would he expect her to leave Tolleson? Could she share him with millions of other women all the time? If she were to be completely honest with herself, in the back recesses of her mind, in a small corner she didn't want to admit existed, she was jealous. Earlier that evening, she'd been possessive. Just the thought of those hormonal women touching any part of Caleb had flipped a switch in her that she never knew was there.

What was it about him that brought out the visceral, irrational side of her?

Chapter Eleven

The following afternoon, after shaving off his beard and sweet-talking Elizabeth into cutting his hair for him, Caleb spent four hours making homemade peanut butter cookies. He then set aside three dozen for the household, one of which literally had Katy's name on it.

Packing up his day's work, Katy and bodyguard in tow, he drove to the police precinct to personally deliver his apologies for the prior night's fiasco. The look on Sheriff Netter's face was priceless as Caleb held out the massive box filled with the still-warm goodies. And then when he announced that they were made from Elizabeth's recipe as Eddie held up two gallons of cold milk, a low rumble of awe rippled through the crowd. Within five minutes of entering the building, he'd not only been forgiven, but reassured that if he had any further problems, don't hesitate to call for help.

They were more than happy to oblige him.

Katy just stood back and giggled, watching Caleb's charm work its usual magic. He stayed and chatted with the police that were there, nibbling at the cookies and subtly finding out where their budget deficiencies were the worst.

And she noticed that he was also studying them. He was watching their feelings, their attitudes and their mannerisms. He asked questions about their jobs and their homes and what it was like to be a police officer. He studied their words, and he studied their body language to discover what they weren't saying.

By the time they left, he'd signed seven autographs for wives or daughters (none of the police, even the female officers, would admit it was for them), and stood for a group photo, taken with the evidence camera.

As they climbed into their vehicle, he pulled out his cell phone. "Hey, Abigail," he started, "I need you to make some purchases." He paused. "I need you to buy ten new police grade handheld radios and twenty batteries to go with them. Don't get crappy ones, either. Make sure they're the best. Get the mikes as well. And chargers."

He paused. "The police station in Tolleson. And leave my name off it. I don't want anyone knowing where they came from, all right?" He paused again. "I mean it, Abby. I know that tone of voice. You aren't going to use this for PR." Another pause. "Too bad." He smiled. "Oh, one more thing. I'm sure Eddie's given a full report about last night's fiasco." He paused again. "During your brilliant damage control, see if you can fool Psycho Fan." He smiled and chuckled before adding "Thank you. Bye."

"So, uh, who's Abigail?" Katy asked casually.

"She's my manager slash assistant slash wardrobe advisor slash surrogate mother. She's married to my security specialist, Todd." And then he smiled impishly, dismissing the subject. "Feel like swimming before you have to go to work?"

A strange normalcy settled over the following two weeks. They swam in the river, read, talked, completed algebra homework, hiked the nearby trails, watched television, and played cards—always together. She was living inside a fairy tale.

He paid up on his rummy bet.

He drove her to class, and then after she announced proudly to him that she achieved a B on her test, he took her straight to the ice-cream drive thru and ordered a chocolate malt, extra thick, extra chocolaty, with cherries.

He chose a random parking lot and shut off the SUV, leaving the radio playing before finally handing her the prize. Happily, she peeled back the lid to the cup and dipped the spoon in the mixture, lifting it to her mouth and reveling in the combinations of tastes. She would miss getting these when he was gone. Not only could she not afford it, but it was much more fun with him there, drinking his strawberry shake.

It was then that she realized Caleb's eyes were glued to her lips, watching her every movement. How embarrassing.

"Why do you always stare at me when I eat?" Katy asked petulantly, digging her spoon back into the mixture.

"Because apparently I'm a masochist," Caleb mumbled under his breath. He raised his volume slightly and replied louder, "I've never seen anyone enjoy the experience quite like you do, Katy. It's enjoyable to watch."

"Well, it's weird," she told him, and took another bite of her cherry chocolate malt. He gasped beside her, and she peeked at him out of the corner of her eyes. "What?" she asked, thoroughly self-conscious now.

"Is that as good as you make it look?" he asked with a strangled voice.

"Would you like a taste?"

She held her spoon in his direction, making sure there was a cherry in the portion. But he leaned past her offering and took his sample from her lips. He kissed her lingeringly, leaving her whole body a pile of mush. He finally pulled back, sitting behind the wheel again, licking his lips thoughtfully.

"Yeah, I can see why you like those so much. They're delicious," he said

He was honoring her promise to her grandfather, waiting to kiss her until they had a chaperone of some sort, or until it would be physically awkward to get carried away—like while they were sitting in bucket seats in a parking lot. He never vocalized it, but she knew without him saying the words; he didn't trust himself otherwise.

Did he know that if he tried hard enough he could probably get her to break her promise? Most likely; her body gave her away whenever he touched her. And so he was the perfect gentleman for both their sakes.

Which only made him that much more wonderful. Like he needed to add anything else to the list of reasons why he was so great. Which was actually terrible.

Their relationship could never work. He was a rich, famous, gorgeous man of the world, while she... she was a country bumpkin who could barely read and worked the night shift at the corner gas station. Soon, he would return to his films, the parties, the "events," and forget all about her and their magical kisses. She was the woman who had helped him recover from his breakdown, and soon, he would recognize he was merely grateful that and be on his way.

For the first time in her life, she tried to build a wall around her heart, so that it wouldn't shatter when he was gone. But every time he did something wonderful, it was a sledgehammer, battering through her defenses.

He claimed he was falling in love with her. Could their two worlds ever really merge? She didn't know enough about his, and he didn't like talking about it. So she formed her own plans. Need information? Research!

On a bright Saturday morning, she woke up early and quietly left the house, walking alone to the library a mile away. Since she didn't have internet access or a phone (or even a computer) in her house, this had always been her source for all things technological. And Saturday mornings were her favorite, because she had the computer lab to herself.

Sliding on headphones, she pulled up a search browser and typed in "Derrick Nelson." She choked when the page loaded, bragging "Results one to fifteen out of twenty two million, six hundred thousand, forty eight." This was a bigger task than she originally thought.

The browser conveniently supplied an image gallery, so she decided to start there. Clicking on the link, she found a page full of little images that she could enlarge by clicking on them. It was weird. This man that she knew so well, the man that kissed her senseless every day, was foreign to her.

Some of the sultry looks he gave the camera were similar to the ones he used on her, but none of them were quite right. In most of them, he just looked like he hadn't been fed lunch yet. Katy had to admit, the pictures did look nice, though. Very nice.

And then she started reading some of the comments from his fans, and her face enflamed. They discussed his anatomy in intimate detail, and what they'd like to do with that anatomy, getting downright pornographic in some places. They bewailed immature fans that attacked him in public, causing his accessibility to gradually diminish.

She read his biography and found that it was mostly accurate, but wholly inadequate. All these people thought they knew him, but they didn't have a clue.

Then she decided it was time to venture onto YouTube, the repository of all things video. Katy typed in his name, and started watching clips at random. Within minutes, she was laughing so hard, she had to clamp her hand over her mouth to stop herself from guffawing out loud and getting herself booted from the library. Her whole body was shaking with the effort to restrain herself.

Caleb couldn't give a straight answer in an interview to save his life. Those poor people would ask a simple question about his work, and within three sentences he was rambling about a lion tamer he once saw at the circus when he was seven. And he talked with his whole body, gesturing with his arms, completely open and expressive with his eyes, drawing out the story until time was up.

The reporters finally figured out that they only had two or three questions at most before they lost control, so they started to ask their most vital ones first. Sometimes it worked, sometimes it didn't. She'd never met a man so adept at prevarication before.

And it brought home to Katy how fully he trusted her, because he never, ever applied the same tactics to her questions. He was always direct... and sometimes verbose, she thought ruefully.

Around that time, she stumbled onto the fan made music videos.

Oh mama!

Most of them were garbage. But she started one that instantly had her glued to the screen with the carbonation running fully rampant through her veins. The music was upbeat, but had the seductive quality of a hunter stalking its prey. As the melody and drumbeat matched the thump of her heart, clips of Caleb started to flash across the screen.

The whole collage of public appearances and photo shoots was timed flawlessly—he'd nod his head, or flash a smile, or lean over slowly, or clench his fist, or kiss the girl passionately at each perfect lyric or beat. At one point, he was walking through a crowd, surrounded by bodyguards, dark sunglasses covering his eyes, and each step was in perfect synchronicity with the bass thump.

When the music faded away, Katy was fanning herself with her hand. Looking around to make sure she was still alone, she watched it one more time.

The next one she found paid homage to his smiles, and for three and a half minutes she watched a compilation of his various laughs and quirks, once again perfectly timed to the upbeat music. The vidder certainly found quite a few examples of him tapping his thigh, or raising his eyebrows, or tossing his head to the side.

He rarely hit his thigh at home, but the more interviews she watched, the more Katy realized it was a nervous tic, when he felt uncomfortable or embarrassed. He did it a lot, actually.

She decided to indulge in one more, titled "Derrick Nelson's Funniest Interview Moments", and the song was "I Feel Good." It was a compilation of every shock, gasp, eye roll, embarrassed cringe and full body guffaw that they could cram into the length of the song. But she was smiling by the end of it, because it was like being with a condensed version of Caleb—the effect only that much stronger for the absence of all distracting details.

Sighing, she forced herself to focus and went in search of more interviews. An interesting pattern began to emerge. With increasing frequency, she realized his name was connected with some woman named Veronica DeWitt. Curious about a possible former girlfriend, she clicked on some links and instantly recognized the woman from Cold Fire, the one that was saved in the end.

Katy acknowledged to herself that she was a little jealous, but that she needed to get over it. Of course, he had a life before coming to Tolleson. Of course, he didn't live the life of a hermit. Of course, there would be prior women. It didn't matter that they were glamorous and beautiful and rich and in his social circle. He had chosen her, right? Sufficiently calm, she followed one more link.

At the top of the page was a crystal clear picture of Caleb, clothes askew, hair in disarray, eyes tired, getting into a vehicle outside of a hotel cabin. Veronica's face peeked out the door, watching him leave.

"Derrick Nelson and Veronica DeWitt have long been rumored as dating. Last night, they shared a quiet dinner at the exclusive NightTime restaurant, and then checked into a hotel. Neither was seen again until Nelson left the following day at noon."

She could have handled this information if her eyes had not fallen on the date the article was written: only three days prior to his appearance in her small, silly, insignificant town. Humiliation and fury boiled through her middle, and the newfound irrational, visceral monster roared in protest. Without stopping to think, without stopping to consider her actions, she ripped off her headphones and stormed her way through the quiet library, headed for home.

That *jerk*, that *creep*, that *womanizer* was getting out of her house, and he was going to do it within the next thirty minutes. He could take his bodyguards and go back to his real girlfriend. Katy was so, so, so grateful that she hadn't slept with the man. The humiliation would be more than she could bear. It was bad enough to be "the other woman," but to have turned into a mistress was unthinkable.

The world around her turned a hazy red color, and all she could think about was how awful Veronica would feel if she knew the truth, and that she herself had been a participant. She should have known that he was too good to be true.

Caleb Smith was going to pay.

****

Caleb didn't deny it to himself, he was pathetic. He missed Katy.

He woke up this morning to a paper taped to his door. "Gone to the library, be back later. Love you, Katy." He folded the note and placed it in his suitcase, keeping the first declaration of her feelings for him safe, no matter how casually it had been scrawled.

Hoping to convince her to go for a swim when she returned, he dressed in his cutoff jeans, and went to find Jerry. An idea had been forming in his mind for a while now, and he wanted to discuss the financial feasibility with someone who had knowledge about such matters, and about the community. As he had suspected, she was sitting at the kitchen table, working at her laptop.

The woman worked too much.

"Hey," he greeted sitting next to her and picking up the salt shaker in the center of the table, idly twirling it between his fingers.

"Hey," she returned, hitting a few more buttons, and then looking up at him. "What's up?"

He paused for a moment before starting. "You've lived here a while, right?" he asked.

"A couple of years now. I moved in shortly after Katy's grandfather died," she answered.

"You know the area well? The community?"

"I guess. I'm not as socially adept as Katy is, but you can't help but know your neighbors with a landlord like her," Jerry told him with a smile.

"Do you think the area could use a theatre?" He peeked up at her to see the sophisticated woman staring at him, her expression unreadable.

"What kind of theatre?" she finally asked. "If you're looking to make money off the venture, I'd have to say that you won't get rich."

"No, nothing like that," he clarified. "Like a community theatre. There could be a children's theatre workshop, where the kids put on the productions, and a youth program for the older kids, and then the regular plays put on by everyone, including adults. You can teach the kids how to do the lighting and stage management. Does the school have an orchestra? They could provide music. Give everyone in the performance two free tickets, and then charge a small entrance fee. Charging money always seems to put an exciting legitimacy on it."

"There aren't any facilities around here for that," she pointed out.

"What if one was built?" he asked. "Do you think there would be enough participation to make it worthwhile?"

She considered the idea for a moment. "You've put a lot of thought into this, haven't you?" It was more a statement than a question.

"Yes," he answered truthfully. "Theatre was where I started. I loved it. I miss it."

"Are you planning on giving up movies?" she asked, not looking him in the eye any more.

He paused before answering, knowing her real question. "I am contracted out completely for the next year," he finally said. "After that, I plan to scale back my workload considerably. If anyone will hire me, I'll probably still do about a movie a year. But it won't be the end of the world if they don't, as long as I'm still acting in some capacity."

He twirled the salt shaker a few more times. "I love it here, Jerry. I finally feel like I'm at home somewhere. I want to stay." He took a deep breath. "So you still haven't answered me. Do you think it would work?"

"Yeah, I do, actually. There are quite a few small towns around here and with the right advertisement I think you could turn it into a real class act. It'll cost you a lot of money up front. How much were you thinking of investing in this project?

Were you going to hire any employees? Where did you want the theatre located? How big a theatre did you want? Where do you want to be?"

"A smallish theatre, with a seating capacity of a few hundred, I think. Location-wise, there was a large tract of empty land over by the park where the baseball game was played, but we'd have to check on zoning. As for money, I'm clueless how much this would cost. And I'm not a businessman, so I'd need a manager."

He looked at her pointedly.

After a few seconds, his meaning began to sink in, and her eyes grew wide. "Caleb, are you offering me a job?" she asked incredulously.

"Yes," he stated simply.

There was a long, drawn-out silence in the kitchen.

"Why?" she asked finally.

"Because I trust you, you're smart, you're business savvy, you've got great style and you already live here, so you won't have to relocate. And... I trust you."

She laughed. "Trust is a big issue with you."

"Yes," he smiled back. "A very big issue. So what do you say?"

"How much are you paying me?" she asked shrewdly.

"Fifteen percent more than you're making now," he answered. "And since you won't have to commute, you'll be saving all that gas. With prices the way they are, I think that constitutes a significant raise."

She laughed. "When would I start?"

"How much notice do you need to give your current bo—"

The kitchen door opened to reveal Katy, grim faced, eyes glaring. All thoughts of Jerry and the theatre instantly vaporized and he was out of his seat, headed for the door.

"Katy honey, what's wrong?" he asked as all kinds of disastrous scenarios running through his mind.

"How's Veronica DeWitt doing these days?"

Chapter Twelve

Cold dread spiraled throughout his body, and he braced himself. "I don't know," he told her calmly. "I haven't seen her in almost a month."

"Oh really?" Katy asked acidly. "So you didn't spend the night in a hotel room with her three days before the end of your last shoot?"

He nodded. "That would be the last time I saw her," he confirmed. "That was almost a month ago, believe it or not."

"I asked!" Katy yelled, her entire body shaking, looking around the kitchen like she was searching for something to throw. "I asked you if there was anything else you needed to tell me! And all you talked about was your stupid money! Like I care about your stupid money!" She glared at him again and backed up as he took a step closer to her. "A girlfriend, Caleb! Why didn't you mention Veronica?"

"Because I didn't think about her," he said, the first thing that came to his mind. "She—"

"Didn't think about her?" Katy was still hollering and she choked in her fury. "I want you gone. Get out of my house. Now!"

He reeled back in shock, as though he'd been physically shoved. His eyes were wide and his hands started to shake. *"What?"* he asked incredulously.

"You heard me. Get out of my house, get out of Tolleson, and go back to LA where you belong. Or go to hell, I don't care which."

"Katy, listen to me. She's not my girlfriend. She's never *been* my girlfriend."

"Whatever you want to call your relationship with her, I don't care. Partners, friends with benefits, I'm not sophisticated or modern enough for that, Caleb. I won't share!"

"Katy, listen to me!" Caleb finally shouted. "I am not romantically involved with Veronica, and I have never been sexually involved with her. And we *both* know there's a difference, don't we?" he asked, a hard edge cutting into his voice.

She wasn't listening.

"I saw the pictures, Caleb. And you even admitted to spending the night together. Just go. Get out."

Slightly calmer now, colder, her omnipresent sunshine was gone. There was wall erected around her, shutting him out, and he felt a piece of himself die. It was as though a muscle in his chest had ripped open.

"Those pictures were staged, Katy." But she wouldn't listen. He had told her the absolute truth, and she flung it back in his face.

Stepping up close, letting his body crowd her, he leaned forward slightly so that his mouth was only a few inches from her ear. "I loved you enough to help you keep *all* of your promises. If I was on the make, would I have done that?"

And then, without so much as brushing up against her, he walked away. It wouldn't take long to pack.

****

"What do you think you're doing?" Jerry asked from the doorway as Caleb flung articles of clothing into his suitcase.

"What does it look like I'm doing, Jerry? I'm packing."

"Caleb, don't do this," she told him.

"I'm not doing anything, she is. She kicked me out, remember?"

"Talk to her! Explain!"

His bag packed, he started to zip it up. "I tried that, it didn't work."

"You didn't give her much to go on—"

"She wouldn't have heard me if I tried, Jerry. You know that. She's got her mind made up and she wants me to leave." He heard the harshness of his tone, and a small part of him felt bad for taking out his pain on his friend, but he couldn't seem to help himself.

"Try harder."

He stopped, breathing in heavily, closing his eyes as pushed his face upward for a moment, trying not to cry in front a woman. It was tough, but he finally got a rein on the physical ache. "Jerry, *every single* aspect of my life is up for grabs. I cannot smile at the assistant handing me a cup of coffee without someone reporting the gospel truth that I have broken Veronica's heart, and slept with the coffee girl.

"If Katy can't trust me, then there's no hope for us. Because it will not go away."

His voice broke, and he knew he needed to end the conversation now. Beyond livid at the universe, he was angry at Katy for reading and believing that garbage in the first place. She wouldn't listen to him. And she wouldn't believe him. And that hurt. He had started to think of the long term, had begun the delicate task of merging their two worlds so that they could be together. But at the first sign of trouble, she'd thrown everything they'd developed out the door.

Katy had told him to go to hell. And it felt like that was exactly where he was headed.

"I gotta go," he said, grabbing the handle of his suitcase.

"Wait, Caleb. Don't leave town yet," she begged.

"Stay out of it, Jerry," Caleb warned as he

brushed past her.

"At least think of me for a second," she tried.

"The job offer is still good."

"I meant Eddie, you blind moron. I was supposed to get another week with him, but if you leave now, I won't see him again for a very long time."

Caleb froze mid-step, his back still to her. "Jerry—"

"Please," she asked again. "Don't go yet. Check into the hotel for a night. Just one night. One."

He sighed.

"Do you love her?" she asked.

"Yes," he admitted. "I do."

"Then give me one night. That's not too much to ask for love, is it? For forever?"

"Fine," he relented. He didn't think he was up to facing the crowds tonight anyway. The house was empty as he descended the stairs and walked through the front door.

****

"You should be ashamed of yourself," Jerry scolded, walking into the kitchen to find Katy at the kitchen table.

The woman had her face buried in her arms on the table. She raised her head to look at her friend, knowing that her eyes were bloodshot, her entire face puffy with tears streaking downward. Her shoulders were heaving uncontrollably. Katy burst into a fresh bout of sobs, burying her face in her arms again. She heard Jerry sigh and then felt comforting arms reach around her shoulders and hold on tightly.

"You're... not... supposed... to take... his... side..." Katy said between her hitches.

"I'm here holding you, aren't I?" Jerry asked. "Even though you're wrong, I'm here with you."

"I'm... not wrong!" Katy said indignantly,

129

recovering slightly. "You should see her, Jerry! She's so elegant... and sophisticated... and beautiful... and—"

"So what this is really about is your insecurity, and not Caleb's supposed infidelity," she pointed out.

"He spent the night with her!" Katy wailed.

"So what?" she asked, unimpressed. "And not that it matters, but he says he's never been sexually involved with her."

"What else are they going to do in a hotel room all night long, huh? Play Parcheesi?" the crying woman asked sarcastically.

"I don't know, really. I think I'd ask him that question if I wanted to know. But you are forgetting that this was *before he met you*."

"Jerry, I'm a summer fling, and you know it."

She heard Jerry's laughter, and it grated. "A summer fling? Katy, I hate to break it to you but if the man wanted a 'fling' with anyone, he could have had one that was much more physically satisfying, trust me. He waited. He waited for you. Think about that."

She let a long pause fill the kitchen, and even though Katy dismissed the argument, those words slowly worked their way around her conscience, slithering through her grief. And then her friend added, "There will always, always be dodgy pictures of him, and people speculating about his life, and making up lies. You have to choose to trust him. You have to take his word at face value. And if you can't, well, it's a good thing you let him go now."

Patting her arm, Jerry stood and left Katy to her misery once again, stopping for one quiet parting shot. "I hope you come to your senses soon. Before it's too late."

For hours, Katy rode the wave of self-pity and self-righteous indignation. Caleb was a lying, cheating, manipulative, no-good jerk who would say anything to get his way. She huffed, she cried, she sobbed, she ate. That lasted until approximately three o'clock in the morning.

About that time, the furious haze started to lift, and she was able to start thinking clearly. Which only made matters worse. Because as she replayed the entire scene through her mind, she could see his look of shock and betrayal for what it was. At the time, she thought it was horror at being discovered.

She didn't even *ask*. Not once. Instead, she acted like a childish shrew, tossing him out and telling him where to go in the process. Jerry was right; this was about her own insecurities. How could a man so universally sought after choose *her*, a stupid, simple store clerk with no fashion sense?

But he did. He had trusted her with his secrets.

"I loved you enough to help you keep all your promises," he said. Loved. Past tense.

Was she too late? Would he ever be able to forgive her? That was when the awful realization set in that she had no way of contacting him. On her orders, Caleb had left. She had no phone number, no home address, no knowledge of where he might be traveling to, and no way to find out. He was gone, forever.

A fresh wail erupted from deep within, choking her, and she heard Jerry's hurried stomps as her friend ran up the stairs to Katy's attic bedroom. Without a word, her roommate gathered her into her arms and rocked her on the bed, as though comforting a child awaking from a nightmare. But there would be no waking up from this.

****

At five in the morning, Caleb was ready to leave. The four walls of the hotel room had closed in on him all night long as he stared at them, and he had to escape. Pulling out his cell phone, he dialed Jerry's number.

"You're leaving," she said in greeting.

"I stayed the night, Jerry. I did what you asked. It didn't make a difference. So yes, I'm leaving."

"Well, you can't walk away without saying goodbye. You owe the rest of us that. You'll break Elizabeth's heart if you don't see her."

"I can't go back there," he said. "I can't face her like that again. I'll say something I'll regret. It's better if I just go."

"She's not home from work yet," Jerry assured him. "Just come over. Please."

He sighed, wishing he wasn't such a sucker. "Fine, I'll be there in a few minutes. But don't think you're going to get me to stay until she gets back, I'm only there to say goodbye."

"Fine," the woman snapped and hung up, cutting him off before he could say anything else.

He felt weary. He didn't want to go back to the house, the one place that had felt like home. The one place he wasn't welcome anymore. A knock at the door startled him, and he looked out the peephole to see Eddie standing there, looking as though he hadn't slept much either. He opened the door to him.

"Jerry's fast with that speed dial," Caleb noted. His bodyguard just shrugged.

"You ready?" he asked.

"Yeah, let's go." He grabbed his bag and followed the man out to the SUV.

The ride to the house only took a couple of minutes, and as they pulled into the familiar circular driveway, Caleb knew that this had been a mistake. The ache in his chest ripped open even wider, bleeding now. When the vehicle stopped, he got out alone and climbed the porch steps, remembering all the times he'd sat out here spitting watermelon seeds, or reading with his legs propped over Katy's on the porch swing.

He swallowed and breathed deeply, trying to

dislodge the lump embedded in his chest. It didn't work. Should he knock? He did, once, and waited a few seconds. But Katy wasn't here, he was here to see Elizabeth, so he opened the door and stepped inside. The living room was empty, and he fought irritation. He'd told Jerry he was leaving town, and she knew that he wasn't going to stick around long.

"Hello?" he called, walking through the room, past the couches where they'd had their pillow fight.

He was near the kitchen door, at the base of the stairwell when a noise caught his attention. He turned in time to see Katy at the top of the landing, staring at him in shock. She looked awful. Her hair was limp and stringy, her face red and splotchy, her eyes puffy. Her nose was red and raw and she was still wearing the same clothes that he'd left her in. She was holding the banister with one hand, and a wad of tissues in the other.

"Caleb!" she screamed at him, bounding down the stairs in his direction. "Caleb, you came back!"

He was going to kill Jerry. He opened his mouth to tell her he would leave when she launched herself at him, flying through the air the last several feet. He braced himself for the assault, but her whole body pounded into him, her arms wrapping around his neck, her legs twisting around his hips.

He stumbled slightly before he was able to catch his balance and he braced himself against the couch, trying not to drop her. His arms were already around her, holding her close so that she wouldn't fall.

"How did you know?" Katy cried into his neck, strangling him. "I can't believe you came back!" she wailed. "I'm so sorry, I'm sorry I was such a shrew, I'm sorry I was a pathetic, jealous jerk, I'm sorry that I didn't believe you, I'm sorry I kicked you out, I wanted to call you but I don't have a phone and I didn't know your phone number and I wanted to call your parents to get it but I didn't have any change for the pay phone and I couldn't remember what city they live in…"

Her words were a blur washing over him, the actual meanings getting lost. All he could process was that she wanted him to stay. That she was going to forgive him for Veronica. He hitched her slightly higher around his waist and clamped his arms tighter around her middle, keeping her glued to him as he buried his face in her shoulder.

"That was the longest night of my life," he finally managed to tell her, interrupting the flow of her babble and he realized that his voice cracked.

She leaned back slightly, just far enough to place on hand on his jaw and direct his mouth to hers. She kissed him so sweetly, apologizing and exorcizing her own miserable night as the familiar electric current hummed through his body. But it was more this time. This time, it wasn't just about the fire. As they kissed an invisible connection reached out, grabbing hold of him and drawing him in. A magnetic force pulled him closer and closer to her, as though her soul had been fused to his, and refused to let go of its other half.

And he knew then that no matter what happened, he would never, ever allow anything to rip their souls apart. He would bleed to death if that happened. *She was his.*

Her legs unwound from around his hips, and she slid down his body until her feet finally reached the floor, forcing him to lean over slightly as her arms were still wound around his neck.

"I love you, Caleb," she told him, looking into his eyes. "I'm so sorry."

"I love you, Katy," he told her. "And I'm sorry, too." He picked her up, feet dangling a few inches off the ground, so that he could stand up straight. "We need to talk. There are still things we need to clear up."

"All right," Katy agreed meekly as they headed for the front door. "Where are we going?"

"Down to the river," he said, finally releasing her so that she could walk, but holding onto her hand. "I think more clearly there."

There was a movement out the corner of his eye, and he saw Jerry standing on the upper landing, peering down at them. "You can name your first child after me," she told him from her perch. "Because you really, really owe me."

He smiled, feeling suddenly lighthearted, despite the impending conversation. "You got it," he promised and pulled Katy through the door.

Chapter Thirteen

Morning sunshine filtered down on them as they walked hand in hand to the river. They were silent, neither wanting to break the peaceful serenity that engulfed them. Occasionally, Caleb pointed out a bird overhead, or a flower he thought she'd appreciate.

When they reached the footbridge, the first thing he did was strip off his T-shirt and soak it in the water before wringing it out tightly.

"What are you doing?" she asked curiously.

He only smiled and stepped close to her. Gently, he began to wipe her eyes and face with the cool wet fabric, cleansing away the dried tears. Then he draped the shirt around her neck, letting the cold compress refresh her.

"Does that help at all?" he asked solicitously.

She nodded, touched by his thoughtfulness. "I must look awful," she grimaced.

He almost denied it. She could tell by the look on his face that the words were in his mouth, but he held them back and shrugged slightly instead. "You're still beautiful to me."

What a nice thing for him to say.

"I'm sorry you were so miserable last night," he said softly.

"I did it to myself," she admitted.

"I should have warned you ahead of time about Veronica."

"I should have listened to you when you tried to explain."

"I should have tried harder to get you to listen."

"I shouldn't have kicked you out."

He paused for a moment.

"Ha!" she said. "I win."

He stifled a chuckle and pulled her to the bridge, walking to the center and sitting down, feet draped over the side. She took his T-shirt off her neck and neatly laid it across one of the handrails to dry before joining him.

"So... Veronica," he started, taking a deep breath.

"I don't care," she told him. "I don't care if you were with her, or not with her. You tell me that you're with me now, and that's good enough—"

"Will you shut up and let me explain?" he said laughingly. "Let's get this out there now, so that it never comes up again, all right?"

"Whatever, but I want it known that you are the one forcing this issue now, not me," she emphasized, pointing at his chest.

"Fine. You get points for being progressive and trusting. Now let me earn points for being forthcoming."

"Go ahead," she said graciously.

"As you know, Veronica and I starred in Cold Fire together, and so our names and our fame have been linked ever since. We're pals because we can feel each other's pain. We've endured a lot together. Neither of us can walk down a street without getting accosted." He paused. "Well, outside of Tollesen at any rate, since people still go to bed at decent at hours here, and I'm usually outside at obnoxious times of the day. But I digress.

"At first, we attended conventions and autograph signings together because it was our job to do so. So our names became linked, and have forever been super-glued together. We've been engaged, broken up, cheated on, cheated with, and even pregnant, on many occasions in the last three years.

"You wouldn't believe how many kids we'd have by now, if any of them were true," he said as an aside before refocusing.

"Her fiancé called off their wedding because he couldn't handle the media coverage. I couldn't get a date without either wrecking some poor woman's life, getting stalked by some really scary individuals..." he shuddered at some unspoken memory. She'd have to ask him about that. "... or deal with women who were only with me to ride the fame in hopes of furthering their social life or career or both.

"So, Veronica and I started going to obligatory events together. It was safe, and we chose to ignore the magazines and the internet altogether. I don't even have an email address anymore," he admitted.

"Two months ago, her fiancé called. She wanted a chance to meet with him without the media circus ruining it again. She called me for help and I agreed. While we were dining together, her ex was able to safely enter the hotel room unobserved. When we returned, they spent the night talking on the couch while I listened to my mp3 player in my own room, reading my script for the next day's shooting.

"The next afternoon I made an obnoxiously obvious exit, ensuring the paparazzi left full of their good night's sleuthing. It took the pressure off Veronica and Micah for a while, so that they can see if they can fix their problems. I didn't care, because at the time, I didn't have anyone for whom it would matter."

He paused, and then cringed slightly. "The next week, she returned the favor," he admitted. "When I disappeared, Abigail set up a photo shoot on her beach-front property with Veronica and the man who has played my body double in several movies.

So if you see pictures of me being cozy with Veronica in a bikini, it wasn't me, I swear it. I was already here. You can ask Jerry, she's my witness."

There was a long pause as the sun slowly rose in the sky. Katy watched the water rippling over her feet, trying to focus her thoughts.

He continued after a time. "I do have a past though, Katy. I've had a serious relationship before, that ended nightmarishly because of my career choices."

She flinched, and he sighed with regret.

"Look," he said, reading her thoughts and understanding her doubts and concerns. "I am going to do my absolute best to keep them all away from you for as long as I possibly can. I saw what it did to Veronica and Micah, and I refuse to let that happen to us. But they will figure it out, and they will find you. And then, for a time, you might become one of the most famous women in the world. And..." he swallowed, obviously leery about this next part. "There's more. I hate to ask this of you, but... I need you to stop inviting people to live in your house."

She scoffed. "No way."

"It's not safe, Katy."

"People are basically good, if you give them a chance," she argued. "I'm not going to stop being me to suit you."

How on earth could he demand this of her? He had claimed he was only asking, but it felt like an ultimatum.

"The people you've run into so far have been your average person, either down on their luck or just basically nice. You've been lucky. The people who will search you out now will have an agenda. They can be sneaky and manipulative."

She shook her head defiantly. "Nobody's going to be interested in a nobody clerk in the backwaters of nowhere."

"No," he said, frustration edging his voice. "They'll be foaming at the mouth to meet Derrick Nelson's love interest."

Katy rolled her eyes. "I'm not going to change."

"Then be prepared for me to do whatever it takes to keep you safe," he warned, almost angrily.

It was the actor side of him coming out, she mused. He could bring on the drama when he wanted to. But he would see, there was no reason for concern. *He* was the person everyone wanted a piece of, not her.

"How do you handle it?" Katy finally asked. "Living under a microscope?"

"I didn't," he admitted. "Well, I did all right for a while. At first it was crazy and overwhelming. And then along the way somewhere, you just come to accept it. But after a while, I was getting more and more closed off from the world around me. It was a strange paradigm. The more popular I became, the more alone I was. I started to go insane, I think. That's why I ran off when I did. It was a nervous breakdown."

"So before... you know... I saw those pictures of you and Veronica together, I saw some other pictures I was going to ask you about," Katy said. She wanted to divert his attention from their semi-argument, she didn't want to keep dwelling on it now.

He moaned dramatically and fell backward, throwing his arms behind his head. "Is this going to hurt?"

"I don't think so. But you do a lot of photo-shoots, don't you?"

"Yes," he confirmed, sitting up again, his mood shifting, lifting, as he let their disagreement drop for the moment.

"Do they starve you before those things?"

He looked at her funny. "Why?"

"Because those poses are the exact same look on your face whenever dinner is late!" she told him.

He burst out laughing and couldn't stop for a full five minutes. Finally, he controlled himself enough to say "What? You mean this one?" and instantly, his lips closed with his jaw ever so slightly open. His eyelids narrowed while his eyebrows quirked and those candy bar eyes bored into hers.

It was a perfect replica.

"That's the one!" she shouted, giggling helplessly. "I swear, I kept wanting to make you a sandwich!"

He unsuccessfully tried to contain his laughter. "Everyone else tells me that's a very sexy look!"

"No, that's not your sexy look, honey. Trust me."

"How about this one?" he asked softly, his smile wide across his face as he stared at her lips and leaned closer.

She gulped. "That's a good one," she admitted, just as his lips met hers. They only touched briefly before he pulled back and caressed his nose over hers.

"How about this one?" he asked again, inches from her face, looking into her eyes with tenderness and devotion, his lips still quirked into a slight smile.

"Oh yeah," she said breathlessly. "That's a good one too." He kissed her again softly. "Those are mine, though," she whispered.

"Yes," he agreed, and kissed her again.

"All they get are the diet looks."

"Absolutely," he promised, kissing her some more. "But you know I won't be able to think about you while at work, if you want to keep this look off my face," he said gently.

Oh, he knew *all* the best lines, didn't he?

"Katy, come to Chicago with me next weekend," he suddenly said, pulling his legs onto the bridge and crossing them, facing her. He pulled her hands into his, and started playing with her fingers. "After the interviews, we could do some sightseeing. It'll be fun."

"I can't afford a trip like that Caleb, I'm sorry," she told him, squeezing his hands.

He looked at her like she was dense. "Katy, I wouldn't expect you to pay for it. I'm not a jerk."

She shook her head. "First of all, that's too much. I wouldn't let you spend that kind of money on me—" he tried to interrupt, but she cut him off. "And secondly, I have finals coming up in algebra and I can't afford to miss work. If I don't go, I don't get paid, and I have bills and college that I'm trying to attend. I'm sorry. Please try to understand."

"I didn't realize that your final was that soon," he said. "Are you ready for it?"

She breathed a sigh of relief. He understood. "I think so. I get freaked out, though."

"Well, we'll study really hard all week. You'll ace it," he promised. "But about this other stuff you mentioned—"

She groaned. He wasn't going to make this easy.

"—let me help you."

"No, Caleb."

"Why not?" he asked, growing frustrated. The grip on her fingers tightened slightly.

"I'm not going to be a kept woman," she said, stating what she felt was obvious. But he snorted.

"Katy honey, being 'kept' usually involves sexual favors. We're keeping a promise together, remember? I just want to make sure that you have what you need. Is that so wrong?"

He was making this extremely difficult. "You are a very generous person," she told him earnestly. "But I won't let you start paying for everything." Especially when she wasn't sure if there would be a "them" in the future.

"You're not going to keep working at the Slurp-N-Go once we're married!" he argued, frustrated. "The stupid money belongs to both of us!"

"Caleb, no one's proposed marriage yet," she reminded him, shocked and trying to hide it with calm rationality. This was very, very sudden, and she wasn't sure she would accept. Despite her inability to live without him for a single night, she couldn't promise herself to him if he expected her to change, to close herself off from the people around her.

But she couldn't deny the effect his declaration had on her heart. It screamed with joy and did summersaults of victory, while her head scolded its behavior. She wanted him to ask. She wanted him to promise her forever.

"I know!" he said in irritation, breaking through her inner struggle. "And you're ruining it by being uncooperative, too."

"Oh," she said, realizing that he had some sort of plan and feeling badly that she couldn't come up with something more intelligent to answer with.

"When is your final?" he asked, his mind busy calculating.

"The Wednesday after you leave," she answered.

"I'll be in..." he cast his mind through his itinerary, "Denver by then. How do you feel about Colorado? Will you visit me there?"

She pursed her lips. "I can ask Carolyn to switch nights, I suppose," she relented, wondering if she could have an answer for him by then. This would take serious reflection on her part. "If she says yes and if I leave right after work Thursday morning that would give me until Saturday night to get back here. I think it's doable."

It was the best compromise he was going to get, and he must have realized that fact because he smiled brilliantly. "Thank you. I'll get Abigail to make the arrangements, she'll organize everything."

He stood up and pulled his damp T-shirt off the railing, holding a hand out to her. She let him pull her up and then followed him off the bridge, to a small grassy area on the side of the river, near a tree.

"C'mon," he invited, sitting down against the tree and pulling her with him. "You need to rest, and I'm not ready to let you go yet."

Happy to simply be with him, she pushed all her concerns over the future to the side and chose to live in the moment. Settling between his upturned legs, she rested her back against his stomach. As one of his hands folded over her stomach, the other reached up and started playing with her hair. "Try to get some rest, Katy. You're beat," he whispered.

"What about you?" she asked.

"I'm right where I want to be," he assured. She smiled and snuggled into his embrace, closing her eyes and resting her head against his chest.

The rhythmic rise and fall of his chest was lulling, and his fingers sliding through her hair soothing. "Why do you always do that?" she mumbled, already starting to fall asleep.

"Do what?" he asked quietly, kissing her head.

"Play with my hair," she clarified sleepily. "It's gross right now. I need to wash it."

"It's one of the most beautiful things I have ever seen," he told her softly. "It was the very first thing that I saw when I looked through those glass doors that first night." He twirled a lump around his fingers, letting it fall in cascade before picking it up again. "It reminds me of a shiny penny." He breathed in deeply with his nose buried in the strands. "And it always smells incredible."

She smiled dreamily. "I love you," she whispered.

He kissed her head softly, tightening his hold

around her. "I love you too, Katy. Now rest."

The birds above them sang her to sleep as his breath softly rocked her in peaceful serenity. Snuggling into him, she followed his entreaty, and gave herself over to the other dreamworld.

Chapter Fourteen

"Lizzy, no!" Caleb hollered from the second story landing, momentarily frozen in shocked horror. "What are you *doing*?"

"Painting," the older woman told him in confusion over what she felt was obvious while gesturing to the wall with one hand and clutching a cream covered paint roller with the other.

Roused from his momentary stupor, he sprinted down the stairs with loud thunder and snatched the roller from the artist's hand.

"Not the beach!" he wailed. "Why would you cover up the beach? Who wants a cream colored wall when you can have palm trees, and waves, and castles, and—"

She patted his arm comfortingly. "It's all right, Caleb. I have a new picture I'm going to paint. It's going to be an Italian Villa."

"But... but... *my beach*!" he wailed again, glaring at the half painted wall as though it was at fault for allowing this tragedy. His favorite cloud and turtle were already gone, lost to the cold void of normality. Cream. Ugh. "You painted over Seymore!"

Elizabeth smiled at him patiently. "It's the cycle, hon. There was a carousel under the beach, and jungle under the carousel. Old things must make way to the new." She held her hand out for him to return her roller, but he pulled it behind his back.

"Why not pick a new wall?" he pled with her, but she was unmoved. "I loved that beach. I was writing a play about that beach. Seymore the turtle lived inside that sandcastle with the starfish Wanda, and they had lots of adventures together."

"When did you name the turtle?" the old woman asked as she fought a smile, letting herself get distracted.

"About ten minutes after the first time I saw him. And you killed him, Lizzy. You killed Seymore."

She chuckled. "I didn't kill anything. Jerry takes tons of pictures of my walls before I start over."

"It's not the same," he said childishly.

She patted his cheek. "It is time, dear. You need to let go. Now let me have my roller."

"Couldn't you have waited until I left?" he asked, pulling the item from where it was hidden and holding it out to Elizabeth with regret. "One lousy day. I'll be gone tomorrow morning."

"Would that have been right?" she asked, looking at him seriously. "Would you have preferred me to go behind your back?"

He clenched his mouth closed and looked longingly one last time at the wall before shuffling to the kitchen. His entire day was now doomed. It was an omen. A person shouldn't wake up to the sight of something they love being desecrated.

He walked through the door to find Jerry seated at the table in business clothes, laptop open in front of her, headset and microphone in place. He opened his mouth but she held up a finger for silence and he snapped his teeth together.

Grumbling under his breath he moved to the refrigerator, rooting for orange juice and listening to Jerry's half of the conversation. It didn't make any sense, and he stopped trying to decipher it. At last, he heard her say goodbye and hang up.

"That was the zoning office," she told him, pulling off the earpieces. "They were—"

"Did you see what Lizzy is doing in there?" he asked, interrupting her as he poured his drink into a glass.

Jerry scrunched her mouth and nodded. "Yeah. I did." Her eyes softened. "I'm sorry," she said, taking him seriously.

"We have to give her some other canvases, so she can leave my beaches alone," he grumbled, taking a sip. "You think she'll design the sets for us? Maybe if we do a couple of big productions a year, like South Pacific, she'll be too occupied to kill anymore Seymores."

His face turned pale and his eyes grew wide. "I won't be here next month, when it's the winter landscape's turn at the hatchet. Jerry, you have to keep Hero and Claudio alive."

His stomach turned as he thought about the two deer nuzzling noses over a snow-covered log being forever consigned to cream-covered oblivion. It just wasn't right.

"I'll do my best," his new business associate promised. "She gets stubborn, though."

Caleb sighed. "What were you saying about the zoning office?"

"That land is technically county land. It's zoned as farmland, and is owned by one Jeffery Hendricks. So, we can either look for something else, or try to get Mr. Hendricks to sell to us and see about getting the land re-zoned."

He sighed. This was way more complicated than he wanted. "While I'm gone, scout out some areas, see what you can find. If you can't locate anything better, then start the wheels turning to approach Mr. Hendricks and sweet talking whoever it is we need to convince to let us build."

"Yes sir."

He glared at her. "My name is Caleb. Or Derrick, if you prefer."

Ted poked his head through the back door of the kitchen, searching the room for a second before finding Caleb at the table. "Oh good, Elizabeth said you were in here. Can you come give me a hand for a second?"

"No problem," he answered, setting his glass of juice on the counter and following the man out. "So what's going on?" he asked, looking at all the items laid out on the grass.

"It's lousy of me to ask you to help with this," Ted said with chagrin, "but Kyle's not here, and I can't do it all by myself." He pointed to the long rectangles. "Tables. I need to get them and the chairs set up. I should be able to handle the rest after that," he promised.

Caleb looked at him in confusion. "Tables? Why do we need so many tables?"

"Katy is throwing you a party tonight," was the explanation. "She's inviting only near and dear friends. Which means, you've got a small crowd coming." Ted shrugged apologetically. "I told her you might not like the attention, but she insisted this was different."

Instantly, his stomach began to cramp. "Who are my near and dear friends?" he asked with trepidation.

"All of your bodyguards," was the answer and a wave of relief rushed over him. And then as Ted continued, he felt silly for doubting Katy at all. "Sheriff Netter and all of the police officers who are not on duty, and their families. The Slovacks next door, because apparently you played football with their boys one day, and made sure to include Little Joey. Some of the kids from the playground who think you are the best jump-roper in the county. Kyle's girlfriend and his band. Jennifer and Emily will be here in a couple of hours."

As he talked, they each stood at an end of a rectangle and lifted it on its side, pulling out the legs and securing the bracers. With that completed, they shifted it to a standing position.

"She doesn't do anything by halves, does she?" Caleb asked ruefully.

Ted only laughed. "No, not our Katy."

They moved to another table and began the assembly procedure. "I wanted to talk to you alone anyway," Caleb started, beginning to feel nervous. This was something he'd intended to do all week, but had never created the moment. Now it seemed that the moment found him instead.

"What about?" Ted asked.

"You are the only family Katy has left. Her grandfather is gone, and you are like a brother. So..." he took a deep breath. "I just wanted to let you know that I plan on asking her to marry me when she visits me in Denver next week."

There was no answer at first, and they worked in silence for a while. Finally, her cousin responded. "You're not waiting very long, are you?"

"No," he answered. "I'm not. I've never felt this way about anyone, and I don't see any use in wasting time when we can be together."

The rush was a risk, and he knew it. She didn't understand what living in the limelight was like. He knew she felt he was overdramatic and overprotective and domineering by asking her to stop inviting strangers into her house. He hoped and prayed she wouldn't have to learn the hard way exactly how deranged people could be.

Because he *didn't* want her to change. He loved her for everything that she was right now. He had to come up with a compromise. There *had* to be a way to make this work somehow. He would find it, he vowed to himself.

"I married Jennifer straight out of high school," Ted told him, breaking into his inner war. "I felt the same way you do. I still do and I don't regret my decision at all. Just don't hurt her," the man warned without looking at him. "Or so help me, your bodyguards will be useless."

Caleb nodded, a half smile creeping over his face. He hadn't exactly asked permission, and that was the closest thing to a blessing he was going to get.

"Teddy!" Katy's angry voice called accusingly to them from the kitchen door, livid at seeing the guest of honor helping decorate for his own surprise party.

"Hey there, honey," Caleb called back cheerfully. "Ted just asked me to help him set up some tables for a Future Farmers meeting tonight."

"Thank you!" Ted mumbled gratefully without moving his lips and waving at his cousin. "I owe you one."

"I'll remind you of that the next time I'm accidentally a jerk to her, and you want to rip my arms off."

His co-conspirator just chuckled.

"Oh," Katy said, placated somewhat now that her surprise hadn't been ruined. "Are you done? Because I was hoping that we could go swimming."

"And the plot to keep you away from the house begins," Ted clarified.

"Should I make this easy for her? Or difficult?" he asked with a smile.

"Roll with it, man," he was told. "Always roll with it. Your life will be so much easier."

"What are you two mumbling about?" Katy asked, walking closer to them.

"He's telling me that the key to happiness is to make sure that you are always happy," Caleb improvised, smiling at her and putting an arm around her shoulder, redirecting her toward the house. "So let's go swimming. And then later, maybe we could go get some ice-cream one last time."

****

Katy was right. This crowd was different. Caleb

was having fun. The tables overflowed with hotdogs and hamburgers and barbecued chicken and potato salad and green salad and fruit salad. One table had an array of desserts ranging from brownies to a cake with "Come back soon!" scrawled across the top. Soda and punch were available by the gallons.

Kyle's band played music and children ran underfoot. No one screamed at him, crowded him, or asked for anything other than his attention, which he gave gladly. The jump rope crowd wanted him to Double Dutch with them. The police officers roped him into a game of horseshoes. Little Joey, standing six foot seven and weighing two hundred and fifty pounds, asked for a game of checkers with childlike adoring eyes.

He talked, he laughed, he danced, and he posed with his friends for countless pictures taken by the official photographer of the evening: Ted. But the pictures were for him this time. He was promised that before he left the following day, he would receive a CD with all of the snaps.

One of the police officers had a video camera and was stealthily moving around the crowds catching the highlights, and Caleb noticed that he and Ted were frequently comparing notes.

He was genuinely sad when people began to make their farewells; these were his friends and he wasn't going to be able to see them again for a very long time. Family by family, they began to disperse until finally, only the Gilfrey household remained.

He started to help clear up the mess when Katy grabbed his hand. "Come with me," she told him. "I have something to give you."

Casting Ted and Kyle an apologetic look, he followed her out of yard and down the street. The night sky was a brilliant quilt of stars overhead, lighting their way as she directed him to their spot at the river. They walked in amiable silence, and every once in a while she'd squeeze his hand.

Finally, stopping beside the water, she turned to face him. "I wanted to give you something," she told him, looking down, shifting her feet. "And I've tried all day, but it's just..." she stopped, embarrassed.

"It's all right, Katy," he assured, dying of curiosity.

"Close your eyes," she instructed.

He followed her command, instantly squeezing his eyes tight. He felt her pull on his wrist and then place something in his hand. It felt like a short length of rope, soft and smooth with a hard piece at the end.

"Ok, you can open them now."

When he opened his eyes, he saw trepidation on her face, her bottom lip caught between her teeth, her eyebrows drawn together with her worry. In his hand was a copper colored object that looked like a woven strap about one and half centimeters wide, connected to a shiny penny. He held it up and let the moonlight reflect off the colors and contours.

****

Caleb hated it. She knew it. This was such a stupid idea. He didn't have a clue what it was. She could see him holding it up in the moonlight, trying to figure out what she'd given him and trying to find something polite to say about it.

"It's a wristband," she explained, shifting her weight from one foot to the other, wishing she hadn't given it to him. "It's made out of my hair. Elizabeth knows a jeweler who was willing to learn, and since I can't go with you, and you always seem so obsessed with my hair, I thought it might be like having a piece of me with you all the time, and since you said my hair reminds you of a shiny penny, I had them make the clasp out of a penny, and I know it's weird and kinda creepy but—"

Her rambling was interrupted by his mouth

covering hers, swallowing the words. She felt one of his hands twist through her hair and spread across the back of her head as Caleb pinned her to him. His other hand wrapped around her back, and she could feel his fist still clutching the wristband as he pulled her into his body.

This kiss was different than any of the others. This one was possessive, almost desperate and as his lips moved over hers, he poured out his feelings—everything he'd been telling her all week long was manifested in this connection. She lost all grasp on reality and had no idea how much time had elapsed before he finally stepped back ever so slightly, clearing his throat.

Her eyes were closed and she felt his forehead lean against hers. His hand was now at the back of her neck, rubbing softly. "It's gorgeous, Katy. Thank you."

"So you like it," she stated, immensely relieved.

"I love it."

"And you don't mind that it's a bit morbid and creepy?"

He chuckled softly. "No, not at all."

"I did some research on hair jewelry," she told him. "They were traditionally used for mourning pieces around the civil war era and Victorian times."

Katy opened her eyes to see a wide smile on his face. "That would be the historian in you coming out," he said. "And while I won't be mourning your death," he told her, "I'll be mourning the fact that we aren't together."

Any breath she had instantly whooshed out. "You always say the sweetest things."

He only smiled that impish smile again. "I practice ahead of time," he teased. "I'm not good at improvisation."

She shrugged, giggling. "Whatever works. It sounds good, at any rate."

"Here, help me put it on," he told her.

She pulled the band from his hand and wrapped it around his wrist, clasping it with the modified penny, then held it up in the moonlight.

"It's a perfect fit," he said a little surprised, but happily.

"Yeah, well," she coughed gently, clearing her throat. "Remember that bracer you were wearing that first night you got here?"

"Yeah," Caleb said. He had worn that bracer for weeks while shooting his last film.

"Well, I borrowed it for measurements," Katy admitted. "I put it back after drawing the template, and I didn't touch anything else, I swear."

He only laughed. "Very ingenuous. Thank you."

"You're welcome."

"I love you, Katy," he said softly, looking at her intently with that same sexy look he'd shown her on the bridge, the one meant just for her, the one that screamed, "You are the most fascinating, wonderful, sexy woman on the planet."

She would have returned the sentiment, but she couldn't breathe at the moment, so she wrapped her arms around him instead, hugging him tightly. He scrunched down a little, wrapping his arms around her waist tightly, and lifting her off the ground.

Caleb carried her as far as their tree before setting her down and then pulling her to sit next to him against the bark. "This is our last night together for a little while," he told her, pulling her hand into his. "There is no way I'll be able to sleep."

"Me either," she admitted.

"So let's talk," he said, leaning sideways and resting his head against hers, looking out over the rushing water.

"All right," she agreed contentedly. "What do you want to talk about?"

"Hmmm," he thought for a moment. "Do you

want to have children?" he asked at last. His tone was almost too casual, completely at odds with the stiffening of his body as he placed the question. So this was very important. She wondered what answer he wanted to hear.

"Yes," she replied promptly and she felt him relax. "I do." She could see his broad smile from the corner of her eye, and her heart leapt with happiness. "I always wanted a big family, to fill up the house."

His smile froze and he swallowed. "How big is 'big'?"

So he wanted kids, just not a whole ton. Darn.

"I don't know, I never put a number on it."

There was a moment of silence as he considered her response. "I think I could handle about six or seven," he paused. "Maybe eight," he was gaining confidence now, starting to warm up to the idea. "I don't think I could handle any more than that, though."

She could tell that he was mentally trying to count how many bedrooms were in the house. The answer was twelve. But she didn't tell him that, he might have a heart attack.

"It'll be a bit of a compromise," she laughed, "but I'll manage, I suppose."

She refrained from reminding him that they weren't even engaged yet.

"How do you feel about traveling?" he asked. "My job tends to be erratic sometimes with locations."

"Can I go with you?" she asked, surprised.

"Yes. In fact, I'd prefer it. It seems like the marriages that don't last tend to be the ones where they spend a lot of time apart." He paused slightly. "And then there's the fact that I like to be with you."

"What about the six—"

"Eight," he interrupted. "I talked myself up,

remember?"

"Eight," she laughed, "kids?"

"They can come too." He carefully considered his next words before adding, "I wouldn't have it any other way."

"Then I think traveling would be fun." She paused before adding, "I've always wanted to visit Europe, and go see some castles. So instead, I bought a bunch of traveling books." She smiled into the night. "I'll show them to you sometime. The pictures are gorgeous."

He scooted down until he was on his back, and he rested his head in her lap. Idly, she started playing with his multi-colored hair, running her fingers through it. "Which castles did you want to see?" he asked.

She began to talk, and he listened intently, letting her ramble and play with his hair. Time slipped by quickly, hours seeming as though minutes. When the sun began to rise on the horizon, he sighed regretfully.

It was time to go.

Chapter Fifteen

"You're moping," Jerry accused from her spot at the kitchen table.

"I'm not moping," she denied vehemently.

"You're moping," her roommate reiterated.

Caleb left fifteen hours ago. Shortly after his departure, Katy had gone to bed and slept for nine hours straight. She then continued to lie in bed for another hour, until hunger forced her down to the kitchen. The next five hours were spent trying to figure out how to fill her time.

For the entire previous month, almost every moment had been spent with Caleb—around the house, at work, before and after school. She'd gotten so used to him being in the middle of everything that not having him around felt wrong. His absence was like walking into a room and forgetting what you wanted to grab. Like there was something on the tip of your tongue, at the edge of your memory, and you couldn't quite grasp it firmly, so you were left with the uneasy sensation that something was simply *wrong*, and no matter how hard you tried, you couldn't fix it.

"Come here," Jerry said, patting the chair next to her and scooting it closer. "I'm going to show you something, so that you won't have to go to work all depressed."

Obediently, Katy plopped onto the chair and looked at the laptop. Her friend was online, with a search engine loaded. "How are you online?" she asked, confused. "We don't have internet access."

"The Slovaks have an unsecured wireless network," Jerry answered as she typed in "Derrick Nelson" and hit "search."

"That's stealing!" she admonished.

"It's borrowing," her friend justified. "I need access on occasion, and you won't let us install any."

"I can't afford it," Katy restated for the millionth time to her pro-bono financial manager. She might not be the one to send out the money for her bills, but she knew that on her Slurp-N-Go salary, she wasn't covering all her expenses and saving for school.

"Well, your stubbornness has forced me to a life of crime," was the answer. "But just watch."

A few clicks on the mouse later, a website titled "The Derrick Watch" loaded. A video clip was available at the top, and the blogger offered a commentary.

"After a month of conflicting stories and unconfirmed sightings, Derrick Nelson has finally re-emerged to the public eye. Earlier today, he was seen in Chicago at O'Hare, arriving from an undisclosed location.

"He refused to answer any questions about where he's been, or what he's been up to. But he's tan, rested, and a few pounds heavier—a nice change after the gaunt, hollow look he'd been developing. Wherever he was, whatever he was doing, it was good for him, which means that it was good for us, because he is back with his charm and smile fully loaded.

"He turned the tables on the paparazzi today, and to get the full effect, you need to watch the video. In this instance, a picture really is worth a thousand words. He handled the situation with much more class than I would have. I'd have flipped them all the bird, and then told them where to go and what to do with themselves. No wonder celebrities sometimes punch these guys in the nose and break their cameras."

The video started and, at first, all she could see was grainy, unbalanced shots of a bunch of men walking through a terminal. Katy thought she caught a glimpse of Caleb, surrounded by Eddie and several other bodyguards that she recognized, but the camera was in movement and the operator wasn't that great at keeping his subject in the center of the frame.

"Derrick!" someone hollered as a small mob of photographers, video camera operators and reporters followed the procession through the crowded airport. "Derrick, are you in love with Veronica DeWitt?"

"Derrick! Over here! Look over here!"

"Derrick! Where have you been? Were you really in New Mexico?"

"What have you been doing?"

"HEY! DERRICK!" someone yelled in a rude, mean voice, as though challenging him to fight.

"Derrick! Did you (bleep) Veronica DeWitt?"

Suddenly, the procession stopped. Caleb and all his bodyguards froze momentarily, and then her almost-fiancé stepped out of the human shield and approached the cameraman, his face becoming larger than life, then blurred as he stood too closely.

"Can you do me a favor for a second?" he asked the man behind the lens, the shot now centered on the green T-shirt he'd left Tolleson in that morning.

"Uh, sure," the man answered, "what do you need?"

"I'd like you to point your camera this way for a second."

Caleb then stepped a few people away and wrapped an arm around the shoulders of a youngish man who looked to be in his mid to late twenties. He was wearing jeans and a hockey jersey and a baseball cap, and the look on his face was pure shock.

"Hello, world. This is my friend... I'm sorry, I don't know your name." He stepped back and held out his hand. "I'm Derrick Nelson, and you are?"

"Chris," the man answered, shaking Caleb's hand warily, casting furtive glances at the camera and looking like he wanted to sink into the ground.

"Chris, it's nice to meet you," the star said amiably, throwing his arm around the paparazzi again. "Now see, Chris here has been following me for the last six months. He's a very dedicated man, spending countless long, lonely, hours outside my hotels and apartments. I feel bad actually, it's got to get very boring since I never go anywhere or do anything. But he always asks me the same question about Veronica DeWitt, and what our relationship is.

"So today, I will clear up this question once and for all. I will give him the answer he has risked life and limb to further his career for." He removed his arm from around Chris's shoulders, and then grabbed his hand, holding it earnestly in both of his, looking the reporter in the eye with full sincerity. "It's none of your damn business."

As Caleb stepped away and allowed himself to be swallowed into the crowd of bodyguards, a cheer rose up from the airport bystanders who had stopped to watch the spectacle.

Katy was laughing so hard that tears were running down her face. "Only he could have pulled that off!" she said between her chortles. "And he still managed not to answer the question!"

"I thought you'd like that," Jerry told her. "But now it's time for you to get ready for work, or you're going to be late," she said, closing her laptop.

Katy groaned, but obediently followed her old routine.

Work wasn't nearly as much fun anymore. The hours dragged by, with only one customer all night long. Her reading was better, because of all the hours she'd read aloud to Caleb, and she managed to complete half her book before Steven showed up the next morning.

She allowed herself a brief pity-party on her short walk back to the house, justifying it with the resolve to be social tonight around everyone else. She would laugh and joke and have fun without once sighing or losing focus. She was not fourteen.

"Katy's here!" she heard Elizabeth shout excitedly, and as she moved through the living room, the older woman rushed from upstairs, grabbing her hand and pulling her to the kitchen.

"What's going on?" she asked laughingly, but didn't receive a reply.

Instead, she was ushered through the kitchen door to be greeted by the largest bouquet of flowers she'd ever seen. Red and yellow roses mixed with purple orchids and baby's breath overflowed the lavender vase. Tied to the center of a giant white bow was a cell phone, with a small card attached.

Pulling off the card she read:

I love you, Katy. I miss you already. Dial "memory 1" – Caleb

Hands shaking, she followed the instruction on the note. Looking at the clock, it was only eight in the morning where he was. Could he already be at his interview? Half a ring later, she had her answer.

"Katy!" he breathed into her ear. "You got it."

"Yes, I got it," she told him, trying to keep her smile and the gooey feeling from hearing his voice out of the tone of hers. "But I can't afford it. I'm sending it back."

"Please don't," he asked softly. "I didn't do it for

you; I gave it to you for me. I miss you. I need to hear your voice."

Drat him, how could she argue that logic? She paused. "I miss you, too," she admitted. "Thank you for the lovely flowers. They're gorgeous."

"Flowers?" he said in mock confusion. "I didn't tell Abigail to include any flowers!" Katy giggled and he sighed. "I love that sound."

"I saw that you arrived safely in Chicago," she told him as she ascended the stairs to her attic bedroom.

"You saw that, huh?" he asked, chagrin in his voice.

"It was wonderful! You are all that is awesome."

He laughed. "I shouldn't have done it. It's going to come back and bite me in the butt, but I was in a lousy mood and that guy has been really bugging me for a long time now."

"Well, he deserved it, the jerk."

"The first thing that went through my mind was 'You are so lucky Katy isn't here!'"

She laughed, flopping onto her bed, sprawling over the duvet. "So what are you doing?" she asked conversationally.

"Getting ready for the Cold Fire convention I have to attend in an hour," he told her.

"What do you do at those?" she wondered, having never been to a convention before.

"Today I will eat breakfast with people who donated to a certain charity, and then I'll take pictures for a few hours. Tonight, I will record a commentary with Veronica for a re-release of the movie. Tomorrow, I'll sign autographs and give a presentation. I think there's an interview or two in there somewhere, but Abigail hasn't given me the specifics. I'm pretty much just going to go wherever she points and smile a lot."

"No wonder you look so tired and hungry in all

those pictures!" she exclaimed. "Do you do this a lot?"

"Last month was the first break I've had in over a year," he said softly. "Oh, if you already saw me arrive at Chicago yesterday," he said, changing the subject, "have you seen Emily's blog yet?"

"No, I haven't," Katy admitted warily. "Why? Did she do something awful?"

He laughed. "No, actually. I thought it was pretty great. She did a really good job, you should check it out. She sent me the link last night when she finished it."

"I thought you didn't have an email address?" she pointed out.

"I didn't. Jerry made me get one for business reasons, and Emily sent the link to her, who then forwarded it to me."

"Oh."

"You want it?"

"It wouldn't do me any good. I don't have an email address either. And despite Jerry's pirating practices, I don't have internet access."

"Will you let me connect the household for the sake of the theatre?" he asked. "If you don't, then I'm really going to have to get Jerry to set up an office in town somewhere so that she can do all the work she needs. Which would cost me even more money for rent and for phone lines and—"

"All right! All right!" she relented, frustrated. "You can set up whatever you want. But I'm still going to use the library," she insisted.

"You are so stubborn."

"Yes, I am."

"You'll give in. Eventually."

"Watch me."

He only laughed. "So how was work last night? Any interesting customers?"

"I had one customer," she told him. "But the

night was long and boring."

"You're going to call me when you go to work tonight, right?" he asked hopefully. "We haven't finished our last book yet."

She groaned. "Must we finish *Zombies at Midnight*? It's gross!"

"It was my turn to pick, remember?" he insisted, unrelenting. They'd already had this argument, several times.

"Well you'll have to do all the reading," she told him. "I put the book in your suitcase."

"I saw that," he said. "And I realized that there must have been some sort of mistake. So I put it in your dresser."

She jumped up and ran to her dresser, pulling open the top drawer. There it lay amongst her socks, the half decayed corpse snarling at her from the cover. She groaned again. "Gross."

"I sat through *Love's Abiding Joy*," he reminded her, for the tenth time.

"At least there was no blood spurtage!" she insisted, and she could hear his unrepentant laughter through the line. "Yeah, chuckle it up, funny-boy. But if I get nightmares, I'm blaming you."

"I promise, next time I'll pick something less..."

"Disgusting?" she offered.

"Sure, we'll go with that. I've got a copy of *Adventures of the Stainless Steel Rat*. You'll love it."

"Yippee," she told him dryly, but with a smile. She flopped back onto her bed.

She didn't really mind reading about zombies with Caleb, if he was right there. It was actually kind of fun, because he had a tendency to get into his roles, and she could almost see him becoming the undead, or the fearful victims. It was quite entertaining to watch.

But he wasn't here for her to watch, and the book was truly awful.

"Well sweetheart," he said reluctantly, "as much as I don't want to get off the phone, you need to get some sleep, and I need to leave for the convention."

"Darn," she said, feeling pathetic over how badly she was already missing him.

"Text me when you wake up," he said.

"I don't know how to do that," she informed him. "I've never owned one of these things before."

"Get Jerry to show you how," Caleb told her. "And I'll call you as soon as I can."

"All right."

"Goodnight, love."

"Goodbye," she said, pushing the "end" button, refusing to listen to the voice in the back of her mind that told her things had still not been resolved between them. She simply missed him,

This was going to be a very, very long week.

Chapter Sixteen

Katy stood on the pitcher's mound with a bucket of baseballs at her feet, and a target pinned to the backstop behind home plate. She needed to think, and the repetition of the windup, throw and the *thunk* of the ball hitting the target board cleared her mind.

In a couple of days, she would be going to Denver, and Caleb would ask her to marry him. Was she ready? Everything had been so rushed. When he was here, she felt like she'd known him all her life. He was brilliant and wonderful and fun and... well... the list could go on all day.

He was gone now, and she needed to think this through rationally. Was she living in a fantasy world? Was everything happening too quickly? Was he only interested in marrying her so that he could consummate their relationship?

Being realistic, she acknowledged that their abstinence probably played a huge roll in his rushing the matter. But that would only be a factor if he'd already made the decision that he would never get any action from anyone else ever again. Which told her how committed he was to their relationship, and to her. Because when push came to shove, there were literally a million women out there who were more than willing to satisfy any need he might have, with absolutely no strings attached.

He'd instructed his agent not to negotiate any new contracts for a full year after the current ones were already completed. He helped her study for her final exams, even when he'd been working all day long. He sat with her on the phone for hours, talking her through math problems just because she was scared of tests.

He was building an entire theater nearby, just so that he would have work locally, and so she could remain living in her childhood home. He was re-arranging his entire life for *her*, so that they could be together. His selflessness and generosity overwhelmed her.

But what if he wasn't doing all that? What if he called tomorrow and asked her to sell her house, leave her friends, and to live with him in his little trailers and apartments as he filmed his movies? Could she make the same choices that he was?

And besides all this was the basic problem of his notoriety and her freedom. She loved people. She couldn't, she *wouldn't*, change who she was to make him happy. He wouldn't love her anymore. But more importantly, she wouldn't love herself anymore.

She pictured Caleb's smile and heard his laughter in her ears. She remembered his anger and frustration when she'd accused him of cheating on his girlfriend, and how decent he'd been while he was angry. Each pitch landed perfectly, creating dents in the plywood.

She thought of losing him, of letting him go. Could she do it? Could she tell him that she never wanted to see him again?

The physical pain shocked her. Her lungs expelled all their air, her stomach knotting while her chest felt like a vice grip had been cinched around it. She had her answer. Losing Caleb was unthinkable. And if he called and asked her to follow him, she would. She'd ask him to pick locations where she could still go to school, but she'd go with him.

So there was her answer. She wanted to marry him. And as soon as the decision was made, warmth seeped into her body, expelling any lingering effects of the previously self-induced torture. There was a rightness to the decision that seemed to align everything else in her life. She felt light, whole, and perfectly at peace.

They could make this work. Caleb loved people as much as she did. He was warm, and caring and kind. Despite his lectures on stranger-danger, he was just as guilty as she was of putting himself out there.

She would make him see, somehow, that this would work and that she was right. And, she admitted to herself, she loved his melodramatic side. She didn't want him to change either.

Now, she was just anxious to get to Denver so that he could ask her.

"Hello," a feminine voice broke into her thoughts, and she turned to see a woman standing on the foul line near third base.

She wore jeans, a grey T-shirt and battered sneakers. She had long, gorgeous blond hair and the kind of figure that made other women jealous. She was smiling and holding a mitt in her hands.

"Hello," Katy smiled with a small wave.

"I saw you pitching," the woman answered. "You're really good."

"Thanks."

"Could you use a catcher?"

"Sure, thanks. My name's Katy," she told her.

The woman approached, holding out her hand. "I'm Charlotte Nelson."

They shook hands briefly before the blonde positioned herself behind home plate and started casting the balls back to the pitcher's mound.

"So are you new around here?" Katy asked loudly enough to reach across the distance between the pitcher's mound and home plate, winding up for another pitch. She didn't recognize her, but maybe she had just moved to Pecos.

"Not yet," was the answer as she caught the ball and lobbed it back. "I've gotten a new job over in Westerbrook, but I was looking to live somewhere more rural. I'm scouting out apartments and housing in the area."

"How's the search going, you find anything you like yet?"

Charlotte grimaced. "The problem with looking for rural is that there aren't a lot of apartment complexes, you know? Most everything available is family dwellings. I might just get stuck staying in the city after all."

"Well, I don't know of any apartments for rent, but I have a big house and lots of bedrooms. You could stay with us for a while until you find something that suits your needs."

"Oh, no, thank you," she responded, tossing another ball back. "I wouldn't dream of putting you out—"

"Nonsense," Katy said. "It's a huge house with lots of space. You might not like us, though. We tend to be somewhat eccentric at times. Why don't you come over right now and check the place out? It's only a few minutes away."

"Are you sure?" Charlotte asked.

"Absolutely!" Katy declared, delighted that she was making a new friend.

****

"Hey Katy!" Jerry bellowed the instant she heard the front door slam closed. "Come here! I found some more pictures of—"

She stopped mid-sentence as Katy and Charlotte walked through the kitchen door. Warily, Jerry swallowed what she was about to say and closed the browser.

"What was that?" Katy asked.

"Oh, nothing. I'll show you later."

"All right. Charlotte, this is my friend Jerry. Jerry, I'd like you to meet Charlotte. She just got a job in Westerbrook, but wants to live somewhere more rural. She's looking for an apartment. Do you know of anything available in the area?"

"I've been doing a lot of realty scouting this last week," she answered, and Katy could see the skeptical look in Jerry's eyes. Her friend was not comfortable with something, and she would be very wary of this new woman. "I can't think of anything off the top of my head."

"Oh well. Charlotte might stay with us until she finds something."

"How nice," Jerry answered, with a smile.

During the conversation, Charlotte studied the room with a strange intensity, as though she were searching for something, and memorizing every detail. Absently, she reached up and rubbed her chest with her left hand, and Katy couldn't help but notice the ornate wedding ring on the woman's finger.

"Are you married?" Jerry asked pleasantly.

"Yes," Charlotte smiled wistfully. "We've been married over three years now. My husband travels extensively for his work, so he's gone quite a bit. The artwork in this house is absolutely amazing!" she exclaimed, changing the subject.

Apparently, the topic of her marriage was a sensitive one, and to be avoided.

A phone rang, and Katy looked to see that Caleb was calling her. The familiar rush coursed through her, and she told Charlotte hurriedly, "Why don't you take a look around the house, and see if you like the place?"

"All right, thank you," she said easily and left the kitchen.

Katy dropped into a kitchen chair and answered her phone. "Guess what!" she said as her greeting.

****

Caleb couldn't help but laugh at her enthusiasm. "Umm... Lizzy decided to take pity on me and put the beach back up?"

"No, I'm sorry. The Italian veranda thingy is coming along nicely."

"Well, you can't blame a guy for trying," he sighed as he settled back on the hotel bed and pulled up his laptop. He was using an earpiece, so his hands were free to type and answer his email and chat while talking.

New houseguest was Jerry's newest instant message, time stamped a few seconds ago.

Male or female? He typed in, feeling the frustration

"I give up," he said, trying to be casual and not ruin her enthusiasm. "What's happened?"

Female.

He breathed easier. He trusted Katy, but she trusted the entire world. So far she'd been lucky, but eventually that luck was going to run out, especially once word of their relationship leaked.

"I met a new friend today. Her name is Charlotte, and she might be staying with us for a while."

He pursed his lips, hating his confliction. Everyone was welcome at Gilfrey's. If it weren't for that universal truth, he'd never have found his salvation. And he was trying to take that away from all those people she would help in the future. "That's great, Katy," he said with forced enthusiasm.

She heard his frustration. "Caleb, it's fine."

He didn't want to fight about it and changed the subject. "You and Jerry are still coming on Thursday, right?"

"Yes, Abigail called with all the instructions. We'll be there. Don't worry."

But he did worry. He worried so much that he'd

bribed his new theater manager to come along to make sure Katy couldn't back out. It didn't take a whole lot of effort to convince Todd to send Eddie as his bodyguard, and the added insurance was immeasurable.

Don't worry, Jerry typed, *you'll get your chance. Were you able to arrange the baseball thing?*

Yes, he answered. *And get the theater tickets, so make sure she has a really nice dress to wear.*

"So how was the flight?" Katy asked. "Or even better, how was the airport?"

You actually want me to take her CLOTHES shopping?

"Surprisingly uneventful," he laughed. "I think they are temporarily afraid of me. There were only half a dozen photographers this time."

Oh come on, it can't be all that bad. I thought women loved shopping. You still have the debit card I gave you, right?

"The convention looked like it was a lot fun," Katy told him. "You looked really good on stage. *Really* good. I noticed you were wearing the wristband I gave you."

Yes, I have the card and don't think for a second that I'm like Livy and afraid to use it, either. But this is KATY we're talking about. She hates shopping. Dresses are a foreign territory for her.

"That's because I don't ever take it off," he said.

I have complete and utmost faith in you, Jerry. If anyone can get her to buy anything, it'll be you. I have to lose at rummy just for the chance to buy her a simple ice cream.

"It looked like you were having fun with Veronica."

Uh oh. He wasn't quite sure how to handle that observation. The two of them had a strong camaraderie, which had been the source of their problems all these years.

Flattery does not make it all better, mister, Jerry warned.

"Doing the presentation with Veronica takes a ton of pressure off," he explained, "so that you don't feel like you have to be a one man show for an hour and a half. It is fun," he admitted. "But I have more fun with you."

He heard Katy sigh on the line. Had he expressed himself adequately?

"Caleb, it's all right. You're allowed to have friends." She paused. "But it is sweet of you to say so."

"But it's true," he insisted. "I wish you could have been there."

Flattery? What is this flattery you speak of, oh wise and beautiful, uber-efficient manager of mine?

"Your fans seemed very well behaved this time. No reports of mauling or muggings."

He laughed.

"Yeah, they generally are pretty good at the organized events," Caleb answered. "The Cold Fire fans tend to be very respectful. It's actually a lot of fun to meet with them, and talk about the story and the characters. And I found out a deal has been cut to adapt it for a television series, so there was a lot of excitement about that."

"Are they going to offer you the role?" Katy asked him, and it seemed as though she was keeping her voice deliberately light.

"They already did," he answered. "I turned it down."

There was a long pause on the line, and he wished he could see her face.

What did you just say to her? Popped up on his screen.

Why? He answered back.

She's shaking all over, and trying not to cry.

"Katy?" he asked. "Katy, what's wrong? Do you

want me to take the job? I don't think it's too late, I can call my agent back and—"

"You keep giving up everything for me," she said with a shaky voice. "Someday, you're going to resent me for this."

His stomach turned into knots. "Oh honey. Sweetheart, listen to me. All I am doing is giving up something good, for something great. I'm not losing out on anything, trust me. I love acting, yes. But I'm so homesick right now for you and for Tolleson and Lizzy and the house that I can hardly see straight."

There was a slight pause before she answered him.

"You really mean that, don't you?" she said, amazed.

"Yes," he responded instantly and truthfully.

He almost added that even if she turned down his marriage proposal, he would still build his theater near Tolleson and live in that instead of the Gilfrey house, because the town felt like home, and he'd be able to see her occasionally. But he refrained.

He heard a door open and a voice cheerfully declare "Wow! You have a gorgeous house!"

Charlotte just came back from a self-guided tour.

The voice was oddly familiar, but he'd never met anyone named Charlotte before and no faces were coming to him.

"Thank you," Katy answered her. "So you want to stay?"

"If you'll have me, I'd love to give it a try."

Chapter Seventeen

Hey Jerry, what does Charlotte look like?

She's in her early 20s with long blond hair, blue eyes and a figure that makes me think I need to start buying cottage cheese again.

Don't you dare, he typed, letting himself get sidetracked for a second. *Besides, Eddie likes you just the way you are,* he added for good measure. The woman described could have been any number of a thousand fans out there.

"Are you ready for your test tomorrow?" he asked Katy.

"I think so. It's kind of scary, though," she answered. "Hold on a minute, I've got to do something really quick."

She's running to the bathroom, Jerry typed. *Why are you worried about Charlotte?*

Her voice. It's oddly familiar. But I can't think of who it could be. Very few people know about you guys in Tolleson, so I don't see how it could be a stalker. I'm just paranoid.

Just because you're paranoid doesn't mean they aren't out to get you.

Haha.

I'll keep an eye on her. There's something... odd about this one.

"Okay, I'm back," Katy said into the phone. "What chapter are we on?" she asked.

She's taking you upstairs to "read." Time for me to check out.

Caleb laughed to himself. *Believe it or not, we*

really read. "We're on chapter five," he answered into the phone.

Whatever. I'll catch up with you later.

Her connection was gone. He closed his laptop and lay back against the pillows, readying himself to spend a few hours with Anne and Diane and Gilbert. Anything to keep the sound of Katy's voice on the other end of the phone.

****

A soft knock at the door interrupted Katy's wonderful dream, and she moaned as she rolled over, pulling her covers over her head in protest.

"Ten more minutes, Jerry!"

She was on a rowboat in the middle of the ocean, and she and Caleb were trying to paddle to an island that was two miles away. But he kept making her laugh with zombie impersonations, causing her to not row hard enough, so they kept going in circles. Two dolphins had just swum alongside to see what the ruckus was, and to offer their help.

"I'm sorry, I didn't mean to disturb you," Charlotte said from the vicinity of the doorway. "They told me you usually got up at noon. I wanted to say thank you for what you've done for me, so I made you some breakfast."

Katy pulled the covers off her face and squinted in the dim light. The new girl was standing just inside the door with a tray laden with food in her hands.

"I'll leave it here on your dresser, so you can have it when you're ready. I'm sorry I woke you up."

"No," Katy assured her, feeling like a jerk, but still half asleep and resenting the fact that she wasn't *all the way* asleep, in her lovely dream where Caleb was sitting next to her and teasing her. "It's fine. I should get up. That looks really good," she gestured to the tray with her chin.

"Well, Elizabeth said you have a test today, so I

thought a big breakfast might help. Jerry said she's driving you to class in an hour."

"Thank you, Charlotte. That was very thoughtful of you."

And it was too. It wasn't the woman's fault that Katy was a lousy, lousy morning person. And noon counted as morning, if you went to bed only five hours ago. Her new roommate turned and left, softly clicking the door closed behind her. Moaning, Katy pulled the covers back over her head. Surely, ten more minutes wasn't going to hurt anything.

Almost instantly, she was back in her rowboat, talking to dolphins and flirting with Caleb.

****

"Katy? Katy!"

Her covers suddenly disappeared, and Jerry was standing over her with her hands on her hips, glaring at her. "I'm up," she moaned, lying. "I was just resting my eyes for a second."

"If we don't leave this house in the next five minutes, you won't make it in time for your finals."

"What!" she shrieked, panic and adrenaline forcing her to instant awareness as she jumped from her bed and started running around her room.

Squeezing into her jeans from yesterday, she yanked a T-shirt from a hanger and pulled it over her head, managing to get tangled in the fabric with her rush. Jerry rescued her, helping to adjust it, and then tossed her a pair of socks and her sneakers. Katy nearly pulled her hair out by the roots as she ruthlessly dragged her brush through the tangles and started to run for the door, stopping only long enough to take a few quick swallows from the orange juice on the food tray.

Within four minutes and twenty-two seconds of being woken for the second time, Katy was sitting in her roommate's car, seatbelt fastened, ready to go. Her heart was thumping and she was breathing

178

heavily.

"We made it," she said, exultant. "Thank you for driving me, by the way. And for waking me up."

"No problem," Jerry told her.

A weird taste started forming in her mouth and she realized that she'd forgotten to brush her teeth. Gross. "You got any gum?" she asked, smacking her lips and rubbing her tongue against the roof of her mouth.

"In the glove compartment," she was told.

Searching, she found a pack of spearmint and gratefully opened a piece and popped it in, chewing enthusiastically. It only helped a little bit. That was when she began to notice a dull ache in her stomach and soft throbbing in her head. Moaning, she grasped her mid-section and leaned forward.

"What's wrong?" Jerry asked.

"I should have eaten breakfast," Katy answered, feeling stupid for not getting up in time to consume the meal so thoughtfully provided to her. "I'll be fine." She hoped.

****

The woman in Caleb's arms was stunning. Her blond hair was meticulously messy in an "I just woke up" way, her overlarge blue collar men's shirt was hanging off one shoulder and draped around her bare thighs. Dark eyeliner highlighted her smoldering green eyes and her red lips were parted slightly, invitingly. And all he could think about, as he projected as much lust and desire as he could manage in her direction, was that Katy should be done with her exam.

It was driving him crazy.

"That was good," the photographer said, snapping more shots. "Derrick, you have a slightly angry, edgy thing going on, I like it. Nancy, turn around and lean into him, let's go for something playful now."

He wrapped his arms around his co-star's stomach and laughed when she flinched. He'd forgotten she was ticklish. She stuck her tongue out at him, all the while the camera kept flashing.

"Good! Just like that!" the photographer encouraged.

"I am starving!" Nancy mumbled to him, not moving her lips as they altered their positions slightly. "When is this supposed to be over?"

"We still have the interview to get through," he reminded her, and she groaned.

"Jeff gets into town tonight," she informed him, and her eyes softened with delight as she thought of her husband. The photographer took full advantage. "When does your woman get here?"

"Tomorrow," he told her, and accidentally let his "Katy" face appear for a split second before he reorganized his thoughts so that he could keep his promise to her.

He reached up and mussed Nancy's hair, and she pretended to be playfully offended and knocked at his hand, scowling at him with a smile. "Maybe we could go out to eat. I've love to meet her."

"I'm sure she'd love that," he said, thinking about how Katy loved everyone. "How about Saturday—"

His phone buzzed his pocket, and he knew that this was the call he'd been waiting for. He wished he could answer immediately, but waited until the photographer stopped to take a breath for a second.

"Hold on," he told everyone, stepping out of the set. "I need a break for a minute."

Nancy was very grateful, and went in search of a protein bar as he walked to the other side of the room and checked his text messages. There were only two words.

I failed.

He felt physically ill. His knees were suddenly

weak, and he lowered himself onto the edge of a nearby crate that had been used as a prop. Rubbing his hands over his face, he forced himself to calm down enough that he felt he could keep his voice even. Then he dialed her number.

He waited impatiently for her to answer as it rang, but the voicemail picked up. Now he was worried. He hung up and dialed again with the same result. She had her phone with her, and it was on, but she wasn't answering. Katy obviously didn't want to talk to him at the moment, and he should probably take the hint and leave her alone.

But he couldn't. There was something inside of him whispering that she needed him, so he tried again... and again... and again. Finally, after the seventh attempt, he heard her voice on line instead of the computer generated mailbox.

"I'm so sorry," she sobbed, heartbroken. She could barely talk, she was crying so hard. Her words were watery and her voice broke.

"Katy—"

"You put in all that work with me, and I'm so stupid that it didn't do any good!" she wailed.

"Honey, you are not stupid!" he told her, wishing he was there in Tolleson so he could make her look into his eyes to see the truth, so he could have been the one to pick her up from class so that she could cry on his shoulder instead of over the phone. "You took a really hard class over a summer semester—"

"Caleb, I know twelve-year-olds who have done the exact same work!" she cried.

"But do you know any twelve year olds who can name every single president of the United States *and* name all the kings of England *and* all of the Roman Emperors? How many twelve-year-olds can recite all of the Declaration of Independence and explain what each of the first ten amendments to the constitution mean?

"You are more than smart, Katy. You are absolutely brilliant."

She scoffed and hiccupped.

"Look," he said, "You can do this. You know the math, I know you do. I've seen you do it. You just have issues with tests. It was an off day, but we'll get through this. Next time, I'll—"

"I don't think there will be a next time," she said miserably, and his heart felt like it was going to shatter.

"Katy Marie Sims," he said sternly. "You will *not* give up. You made your grandfather a promise, and you are *not* going to let him down. Someday, I will be sitting in that audience holding that framed picture you keep on your dresser, and I'm going to hold it high so that he can see that diploma placed in your hand."

His voice had softened as he spoke, and he heard her sobs quieting slightly.

She hitched a few times. "It was my own fault that I failed," she said quietly. "I—"

"Derrick, we need to get back to work," someone called and held up his hand without looking. He was not going to end this phone call until she was calmed down.

"I couldn't answer half the questions," she said. "I couldn't concentrate. I had this massive headache and my stomach felt queasy."

"Are you sick?" he asked worriedly. "Maybe your professor will let you retake the exam, if you explain."

"Not this instructor," she told him. "It was my own fault, though. I was so stupid. I didn't wake up in time to eat breakfast so all I got was a few swallows of orange juice that had been sitting on my dresser for an hour before I had to run. I think I made myself sick."

"Stop calling yourself stupid!"

"Foolish, then," she corrected. "And what's really bad is that Charlotte had taken the time to make and bring me breakfast in bed and everything, and I fell back asleep and didn't eat any of it."

"You worked all night, honey. You were tired. Don't beat yourself up for falling back asleep."

Katy sighed. "I didn't want to wake up," she informed him. "I was dreaming about you."

He smiled, liking that she thought of him even in her subconscious. "Oh yeah? What were you dreaming?"

"That you were impersonating zombies... and talking to dolphins."

He wasn't sure if he was allowed to laugh yet or not, so he pulled the phone away from his head so that she couldn't hear his snicker. "Really? Very interesting," he said when he finally had himself controlled.

"You're at work, aren't you?" she asked suddenly. "You had an interview with some magazine today, didn't you? Right around now?"

"Yes, I did. With Nancy Whitmore, the leading lady of the last movie I shot. We were doing the photo-shoot when I got your text."

She gasped. "You mean they are all waiting on *me*?"

"Well, technically yes," he said, looking up and surveying the area. He spotted Nancy on the other side of the room, indulging in a sandwich. She'd been hungry often lately. Very often. "Nancy doesn't mind, it gave her a moment to eat."

"So I was right! They *don't* feed you guys enough!"

He laughed. "She's been extra hungry lately. A lot."

"Oh!" Katy gasped, catching his sentiments.

"Yeah, that's my guess too. But she hasn't said anything yet. By the way, she wants to meet you, and invited us to dinner with her and her husband."

"I think that would be fun," she answered, breathing deeply.

He paused for a second. "Are you all right?" he asked. She sounded better, but he wanted to make absolutely positive.

"Mostly," she answered, sounding infinitely calmer. "I'm still a little depressed. And even though I've eaten dinner, I still have that headache and I'm a little nauseous."

"Maybe you should call in sick to work tonight," he told her. "You need to take care of yourself. I wish I could be there."

"I'll see you tomorrow," she assured him. "And I can't call in sick tonight."

"Then call me when you get to the store."

"All right," she promised. "Your phone bill has to equal the national debt by now."

"That's all right, sweetheart."

There was a slight pause. "Thank you, Caleb," she whispered.

"For what?" he asked, confused. He hadn't done anything.

"For being annoyingly persistent. I was embarrassed to talk to you. But you made everything livable again."

"You're welcome," he told her, glad that he could help in some small way. "It's only because I love you, you know."

"I love you, too," she returned. Then she sighed and became stern. "But listen here, young man. You are being very unprofessional right now. You need to get off the phone with personal business, and get back to work!"

"Yes, ma'am," he snickered. "Slave driver."

"You got that right!" She imitated the crack of a whip, causing him to laugh before they hung up.

As soon as the "end" button was pushed, he

looked up to the set to find the make-up artist hovering and he sighed. Soon. Tomorrow at this time, Katy would be here, and he could properly take her mind off her troubles.

Chapter Eighteen

Three days. Three perfect days. Katy and Jerry arrived in Denver Thursday afternoon, to be met at the airport by Abigail and driven to the hotel. She'd never stayed in anything so fancy. There was actually a "parlor," with a piano in it, and a full living room set of furniture, and a dining room table and chairs and a little kitchenette. There were two bedrooms, and Caleb gave them the ultra-fancy one with the mahogany king sized bed and gold and brown duvet, while he stayed in one much less magnificent.

That first day, they remained in the hotel room, playing cards and board games, reading, and eating. Lots and lots of eating. She wouldn't be surprised if she went home ten pounds heavier. But oh, it was pure bliss. They could have continued those activities for her entire visit, because all she cared about was being with Caleb.

But bright and early Friday morning, she was woken at a ridiculously early hour and whisked away to a train station, where she and Jerry were treated to a train ride on a steam locomotive through the mountains. She felt like a little kid as she craned her neck in every direction to see everything all at once. It was like stepping back in time, participating in history.

Keeping with the historic theme, when the train ride was over they were taken to a museum and she was allowed to move through all the old west exhibits as slowly as she wanted, without anyone coughing at her to hurry up and move along. Caleb patiently stood beside her and listened as she read each and every placard. The poor man was probably bored to tears, but he smiled and pointed out things he felt would interest her, so she accepted the gift for what it was, hoping that she could return the favor someday.

Occasionally, a fan would stop and apologetically ask for an autograph from "Derrick." He smiled, signed whatever they handed them, and posed for pictures graciously. She was worried at first, that he would get upset, because he was so intent on spending every second with her. But he retained his jovial mood, putting the fans at ease and joking with them.

That evening, she was instructed to put on the fancy new dress Jerry had bullied her into buying, and they all were treated to an evening at the theater. Katy had never experienced a performance live, and it was unforgettable. This was Caleb's world, and she immersed herself in the story and the fantasy and the costumes. Afterward, they drove to the kind of restaurant where the waiters wore suits and ties and put the napkin on your lap for you. She was plied with salad and course after course of seafood. She lost track of how many different types of shrimp she'd eaten. It was all heavenly.

But today, Saturday, was by far the best day of them all.

Caleb had blindfolded her in the hotel room and, holding his hand, she followed him through the corridors and into the elevator. She was led outside, and gently guided into a vehicle, though she couldn't guess which kind since they'd been using a different one every time they left their lodgings.

The trip itself took a while, with Caleb occasionally reminding her not to peek while he kept up the conversation. She was completely lost and disoriented which was, no doubt, his goal. At last they stopped. Katy heard him exit the vehicle, and open her door. His hand was soft and warm on hers as he helped her out.

As she followed his slow progress, she heard the grinding screech of metal and realized they were passing through gates of some kind. They climbed a few steps, descended a few steps, and went through another gate before their pathway was apparently clear.

Finally, at long last, they stopped. Caleb turned her around so that she faced him, and he removed the blindfold. The first thing she saw was his smiling face, looking extremely happy and pleased with himself. The next thing she saw was the field they were standing on. On a pitcher's mound.

She was on a pitcher's mound in a stadium. A real stadium. The empty bleachers stretched upward, the grass of the outfield perfectly manicured, the foul lines meticulously chalked. At her feet sat a giant bucket of neon green practice baseballs and her beloved, well-worn glove. She and Caleb were completely alone. Not even the ubiquitous bodyguard was anywhere in sight.

Her heart stopped.

"Caleb..." she stuttered, speechless. "Caleb... how?"

"I rented it for the day," he told her proudly. "We lucked out; the Rockies had away games this weekend."

"You *rented* it?" she asked incredulously, shocked. "You *rented it?* How? That had to cost a fortune!"

He rolled his eyes and shrugged. "Don't ruin this for me. Just say 'wow' and be happy. Please?"

"Wow," she said. "And I am happy. This...this is...incredible."

His impish smile returned and he almost looked

like a little boy, dancing from foot to foot. "I'm going to try to catch for you," he told her. "But my experience is limited to a sand-lot situation from back when I was a kid. So be nice."

"Do you have a glove?" she asked.

"I've got a catcher's mitt over there at home plate, along with a mask. And I've got a regular glove I borrowed off Eddie."

"How about a bat?"

"We have a bat," he assured her. "Although you'll strike me out every time, I've no doubt."

"You thought of everything," she said, throwing her arms around his neck.

"I wish I could take credit," she said, hugging her tightly. "I asked Jerry, and *she* thought of everything." As if by magic, he produced her green Tolleson team baseball hat.

Katy only laughed, grabbing the headgear and situating it on her head, pulling her hair into a ponytail through the adjustment strap. "But you took the time to ask someone, which counts as the same thing. Grab your glove; let's catch for a little while."

"Yes, ma'am," he said saluting, and ran off to retrieve the item.

All morning, and late into the afternoon, they played together. They played catch, and then she pitched for a while before succeeding in convincing him to try batting. She took it easy on Caleb, specifically pitching so that he could hit the ball, and chased him around the bases. Then, after much pleading on her part, she convinced him to toss a few balls in her direction so she could bat for a while.

Finally, he declared lunchtime and told her to go stand in the outfield while he ambled off to a large ice chest she just barely noticed resting quietly near a dugout. The thing was so huge it had a handle on one side, and wheels. He dragged the cooler across the infield and joined her in the grass.

Together, they opened the lid and peeked inside. The hotel had provided everything. There was a large blanket, cups, paper plates and plastic utensils. For food they had packed lemonade, fried chicken, potato salad, and fruit.

They laid out the blanket and sprawled across it Roman style, ignoring the plates provided and eating directly from the containers and passing the lemonade jug back and forth between them. Stuffed, and deciding she couldn't eat another bite, Katy moaned as she rolled over onto her back to look up to the puffy clouds above them.

"I see a sailboat," she informed him. "What do you see?"

But instead of turning onto his back and joining in her game, he leaned over her, propping himself up with a hand braced near each of her shoulders. His face only inches from hers, it was filled with tenderness and nervousness.

Her breath froze as he opened his mouth, while her heart began to race.

"Katy, marry me?" he said in the form of a question, and she could almost hear the unspoken "Please" at the end of it.

He searched her face, and she tried to tell him "yes" but air still wouldn't fill her lungs so that she could answer him. Helpless, she nodded as she stared into his eyes. For a brief second, his whole face turned into triumphant joy, lighting his eyes as his smile grew wide. But as quickly as it appeared, the triumph was gone, and the nervousness returned.

He sat up a little bit, putting some distance between them as he sighed and ran his fingers through is hair. "That was the easy question," he told her, looking away and refusing to meet her eyes. "I was eighty percent sure what your answer was going to be."

She wasn't sure whether to be insulted that he said asking her to marry him was easy, or to be miffed that he was only partially sure what she was going to say. But he continued before she could express either of those mixed emotions.

"I'm about to ask you something very difficult. And I'm hoping that you'll take a little while and think about it. It's huge."

Now she was worried. He was going to ask her to close Gilfrey's doors, and she would have to tell him no.

He cleared his throat. "This last week has been killing me. I'm pathetic, I know, but I'm so homesick that I just want to quit everything and go home. I can't do that. So I am going to be very, very selfish and ask you to come with me." He paused for half a second, taking in a deep breath. "For one year, that's it. I have a week with nothing scheduled in the middle of August. If we got married then, you could travel with me. You wouldn't have to give up school, I'm sure we could enroll you in some online courses, or correspondence courses, or both. I could help you, and you'd have more time to study, since you wouldn't have to work," he continued, trying to throw out every possible positive factor he could think of. "You could visit Tolleson whenever you wanted, it's not like you'd be chained to me, and I have to go back sometimes to deal with the construction of the theater—"

Was that it? "The middle of August?" she asked him, interrupting as the relief poured through her.

"Yes," he answered hesitantly.

"That's two weeks away."

"I know."

She took a deep breath and sat up, forcing him to scoot back a little further. "First of all, yes," she told him, putting a hand on his cheek. "I'll go with

191

you."

He looked like he wanted to grab at her answer and run with it, but instead he said "Katy, this is a big decision. You need to think about this for a little while. Maybe you should talk to Jerry or Lizzy—"

"I already have thought it through, Caleb," she interrupted him again. "And this isn't something I need to discuss with other people. I spent a great deal of time thinking about it, as a matter of fact. And my answer is yes."

She was able to see his wide, joyous smile before his lips met hers, and then she wasn't able to see or think of anything else for a long time. She poured everything she was feeling into her response; desperately trying to tell him how happy he made her every single day—how much she loved him.

Before she was ready, he pulled back slightly and leaned his forehead against hers.

"Is two weeks enough time to plan?" he asked her belatedly.

"We could jump on a plane and go to Vegas right now," she answered, knowing that, as much as she wanted to, she couldn't. He agreed, apparently.

"What a nice thought," he sighed. "But you have to give your job two week's notice, and it would kill my mom."

He reached behind her, digging into the cooler, and then produced a small green jewelry box. He opened it up and held it in front of her to reveal an engagement ring. The diamond was small and inlaid as the centerpiece of an open, gold rose. Delicate gold leaves draped on each side, morphing into the band that would surround her finger.

"Oh, Caleb, it's gorgeous," she breathed.

"It was my grandmother's," he told her, taking it out of the box and lifting her hand to slide it on. "I was going to buy you a new one, with a huge, obnoxiously large stone. But the more I thought about it, the more it felt wrong."

"I love it," she told him, throwing her arms around his neck. "And it fits perfectly."

He smiled impishly and shrugged. "I'd like to say it was cosmic destiny, but I have to admit that I got your ring size from Lizzy. It just came back from the jeweler's yesterday evening."

She laughed. "I wondered what was taking you so long to propose!" she exclaimed. "I was afraid you were going to wait until we were in the airport getting ready to leave!" She paused for a second and shrugged. "Or that you changed your mind."

"Absolutely not!" he exclaimed before kissing her again. "As much as I would love to sit here all day with you, I actually have to work tonight for a couple of hours."

"Darn," she said, disappointed. "Another photo-shoot?"

"No, a radio interview," he answered, getting up and packing away their lunch. "It'll be live. Those always make me nervous."

"You'll be great," she told him. "You always are. You could belch the national anthem, and you'd still have the girls in a swoon."

He rolled his eyes, grabbing her hand and leading her out of the park. "I think you overestimate my charming abilities."

"I think you underestimate your appeal," she returned. "What station?"

"You're not going to listen to it, are you?" Caleb asked dejectedly.

"Of course I'm listening to it!" she informed him and he groaned. "We all will."

"Great," he mumbled. "Just wonderful."

She simultaneously tip-toed and pulled him down closer to her with their joined hands and kissed his cheek. "You don't really mind, do you?"

He cast her a glance from the corner of his eyes

and sighed dramatically. "No, I guess not."

Smiling, she followed him out of the park, excited to get back to the hotel and show off her new ring.

Chapter Nineteen

"Katy, you have to see this," Jerry called from the kitchen table.

Intrigued, she left the sink where she was washing dishes and stood behind her friend to look at the laptop. At first glance, she gasped, losing all her air. It was "The Derrick Watch" again and right at the very top, crystal clear and nearly as big as the screen, was a picture of Caleb kissing her right outside the train depot while they waited to board the steam locomotive.

"Oh my gosh!" she whispered breathlessly, sinking into the chair beside Jerry.

She remembered that kiss. She remembered how it felt, and looking at it from the outside didn't seem to change the effect on her inner organs at all. It was like reliving it again. She cleared her throat, trying to form a coherent reply.

"Derrick Dating Mystery Woman!" was written in bold letters at the top of the blog.

Whoever had taken the pictures had done a better job of capturing their vacation than they had. Jerry slowly scrolled through all the snapshots, giving time for them to read the captions. There were countless pictures: Caleb looking at her with adoration, Caleb with his arm around her shoulders, his wristband getting lost in her hair, Caleb whispering in her ear, Caleb pointing to an exhibit in the museum, Caleb laughing with her, Caleb holding her hand outside the restaurant, and Caleb kissing her.

Someone must have stalked their every move, because there were countless kisses—casual, flirty, intimate—for the entire world to see and judge. Her first thought was that she didn't realize they'd been that demonstrative and it must have been annoying to Jerry and the others. But that feeling only lasted for a split second before the embarrassment began to emerge.

The site even had pictures of Caleb kissing her good-bye at the airport, and they'd only been back home for a few hours. The only moments missing from the collection were from the stadium, and she sent a silent "thank-you" to whoever was listening to her and orchestrated that small miracle.

Someone had gotten close enough to zoom in on her ring at one point, and one giant picture was of her left hand, their fingers intertwined.

The caption stated "Is this was it appears to be?"

"Scroll down to the comments," she ordered.

"Oh no, you're not going that route," her roommate denied.

Her teeth grit together, Katy answered. "If you don't scroll down, I will go to the library and look for myself."

Scowling, Jerry did as she was told, muttering "You're being silly," under her breath. "Masochist."

She didn't care. If her love life was going to be public knowledge, she was going to find out what all those "fans" were saying about "Derrick" now that he was apparently involved with someone. Would he lose his following? She knew that he hoped so, but she didn't want to be the cause of him losing jobs... which he might if he lost popularity.

The comments were all over the map. Some were happy for him, congratulating him and thrilled that he seemed so happy. Others were angry that he'd treat Veronica that way, cheating on her with "a skank-whore." That note made her laugh for some reason.

The comments about her were just as eclectic as those about Caleb. Some felt she was pretty, but not good enough for him. Some thought she was "an ugly tramp." Some felt that she looked nice enough, and that the other jealous harpies should leave her alone because she obviously made him happy, and when was the last time you saw a smile like that on Derrick's face?

There were a ton of "Oh, I wish I could be in her shoes!" comments.

There was speculation about his wristband: several people caught the similarities between her hair and his new article of clothing that he hadn't been seen without since his re-emergence into society. Some thought it romantic, others felt it was pathetic and prophesied that their relationship wouldn't last longer than a month or two.

Katy wasn't sure how she felt about their observations, and realized that she would be following Caleb's example, and not reading them in the future. She would definitely develop fewer ulcers that way.

****

"I need to talk to you," Jerry said in a grim voice.

Caleb sat back against his pillows on the bed of his hotel room and refrained from telling her that he had already figured that part out since she'd, you know... called him. His theater manager didn't sound like she was in the mood for flippancy.

"What's up?" he asked instead.

"Katy keeps getting sick," she informed him. "She just threw up for the third day in a row."

"Why hasn't anyone told me?" he asked angrily. "Get her to a doctor!"

"She won't go. She keeps insisting it's the flu, and it only lasts for a few hours every day, some days longer than others. If I didn't know better, I'd ask her if she was pregnant."

"I can promise you, she's not," he answered dryly. "The flu doesn't keep going away and coming back, Jerry."

"I know," she said. "I think…" she paused. "Look, I don't have any proof, but Charlotte is really creeping me out. The woman has a strange vibe to her, you know?"

"Are you telling me that you think Charlotte is poisoning Katy?" he asked incredulously, disbelievingly.

But Katy's illness before the Denver trip suddenly took on a whole new meaning. "Charlotte" had cooked her breakfast. After drinking a portion of the juice provided by "Charlotte," Katy became moderately ill.

All the blood drained from his face, and he was grateful that he was already sitting on his bed, or he'd have dropped to the floor. If Jerry was right, then there was a distinct possibility that the only reason Katy was alive was because she had fallen back asleep that morning, and didn't eat her whole meal, or have more than a few swallows of that juice.

He gulped and started praying for the first time in years.

"I don't see how she can. I don't let her cook at all, and I keep an eye on her. But…I don't know," Jerry said, and he realized that it had only been a second since he'd spoken, not the hour that it had felt like as his thoughts and emotions chased each other.

"How could anyone have found out about Tolleson?" Caleb asked. "Or about Katy? We weren't public until five days ago, and no one even knows her name yet!"

"It's not like you guys were a national secret," Jerry reminded him. "People around here saw you often enough. Casual conversation, word gets out, someone hears it from someone's best friend's cousin..."

Caleb sighed and rubbed his eyes. "Have you called Sheriff Netter?"

"What am I supposed to tell him?" she asked ruefully. "'I think there's a chance Katy's new roommate is trying to kill her because she's really creepy'? Come on, I need more than that."

"All right, all right. I'm calling Todd to send someone down there. In ten days, we're getting married, and then Katy will be out of there."

"Thank you. I tried to talk to her about this, but she thinks I'm crazy," Jerry grumbled.

"It *does* sound crazy, Jerry. And if I wasn't paranoid myself, I'd be right there with her, telling you everything was fine. Why hasn't she said anything when we talk on the phone?" Caleb asked.

"She doesn't want to worry you. And she'll get very mad if she finds out that I told you."

"It figures," he grumbled. "Look, just keep her safe. I'm calling Todd."

He hung up, dialing the number for his security specialist, and explained to him the entire situation.

"I need you to get someone out there as soon as possible. I don't have any proof, but it sounds like she's already gotten one good attempt in, and is working more subtly this time. I don't want her to succeed."

"She won't," Todd assured him. "I can have someone out there in an hour."

Caleb paused. "So soon?" he asked doubtfully.

"I took the liberty of setting up a satellite office in Westerbrook when I learned what your long-term plans were going to be."

"You deserve another raise," Caleb told him in awe.

"You'll change your mind when you see what

that satellite office is costing you," his security specialist warned.

"Not if they take care of Katy. Thank you."

"Why doesn't she evict this woman? Does she know what's going on?"

"Jerry's tried to talk to her, but she won't believe it and Katy won't evict anyone." He paused, realizing this statement wasn't entirely true, but he wasn't going to get into the details of his love life right now. "This might just be paranoia on our part."

"Better safe than sorry."

"That's my thoughts exactly. Thank you Todd." He paused again. "I don't suppose Eddie is available again, is he?"

"I'll ask him," his advisor replied. "Any particular reason?"

"He does his job well." No harm in getting brownie points with Jerry, right? "How long will it take him to get there?"

"He's on another assignment right now, but I can have him there in a day or two."

"Thanks," Caleb answered, relieved and worried at the same time as he hung up, dialing Katy's number.

****

Katy was in the bathroom with her face stuck in the toilet bowl and her stomach heaving when she first heard the ringing that declared Caleb was calling. Just wonderful. Past experience told her that he wouldn't stop until she answered. When at last her muscles slowed their contracting, she rinsed her mouth out and hoped that she wouldn't have to race to the bathroom again soon.

"Hello!" she said as brightly as she could, flinching as the searing pain shot through her skull. She flopped onto her bed and breathed heavily.

"What's wrong?" he asked immediately, concerned.

200

His greeting made her realize she could never go into his line of work, but she tried again anyways. "What do you mean?" she asked innocently.

"What's wrong Katy? You don't sound so well."

"What a way to greet a woman," she grumbled.

"Talk to me. What's wrong?"

She growled, frustrated. "I've got a touch of the flu, that's all. It's nothing to worry about. The wedding plans are moving forward, your parents and Livy will be able to come, Jerry is taking me shopping tomorrow for a dress—"

"What I care about is how you are feeling," he interrupted. "We can get married in our jeans, and the guests can eat beanie weenies for all I care."

She groaned at the mention of food and had to breathe deeply a few times to ward off the nausea. "Please... don't talk about eating right now."

"Go to the doctor," he insisted.

"No, I can't afford it!" she insisted right back, and tense silence punctuated her stubbornness.

Finally, Caleb spoke. "Be glad I'm not home right now, or I'd drag you there myself."

"Are you always going to be this bossy?" she asked, irritated.

"When it comes to your health, yes," he returned just as irritated. "Please," he begged, changing tactics. "Humor me. Let Jerry drive you to the doctor's tomorrow."

"Fine," she snapped, wanting to throw the phone.

Her head hurt, her stomach hurt, her muscles ached all over and she felt like a wet dishrag and he was being a bully. Planning for your wedding was supposed to be fun. It was supposed to be hectic and nerve wracking, but enjoyable. But right now, she was seriously considering Caleb's "jeans" idea. Who cared about stinkin' flowers anyway?

He sighed, knowing how much he'd frustrated

her. "Todd is sending Eddie down to hold the fort until the wedding," he told her, and she spared a moment to be happy for Jerry. "We're worried that people will find out the location and time, so we want to make sure you guys are safe."

"All right," she agreed.

"Until Eddie can get there, Todd's going to send another guy out. Please, please, please, listen to him. He's there for your protection."

"All right," she agreed again. She'd get irritated at his over-protectiveness tomorrow. Right now, she just wanted to sleep. But she wanted to keep talking to him. "Caleb?" she asked pathetically.

"Yeah, sweetheart?"

"Can you read to me for a while?"

"No problem," he answered softly.

She turned out her light, climbed under her covers and hit the speakerphone button, laying it next to her head. Just as she was finished adjusting, Caleb's voice began to lull her to sleep to the prose of *Tales from the Grave.*

Chapter Twenty

Stretched out on her bed with the sunset peeking through the cheerful curtains, Charlotte carefully turned this newest problem over in her mind, considering her options and how to counter this latest hurdle. It was like a game of chess, and she had no intention of losing. Her objective *would* be attained.

Weeks of careful planning were about to be destroyed, just as she was so close to the end and fury simmered in her stomach. It was a familiar, comforting, warm fury, her constant companion and the only thing she could trust anymore. *He* wasn't trustworthy. He used her, and then threw her aside. He openly mocked her love with his infidelity.

When Derrick had disappeared after filming *Nothing and Nowhere*, she'd meticulously followed every rumor, every clue. He thought he'd confuse her, tease her, with that phony story of him vacationing with Veronica on the beach, but it didn't work. Everyone else was stupid, but she knew it was a fake.

And then he'd been spotted at that county dance in New Mexico, and she had her lead. He disappeared again and everyone was sure he'd gone to LA, but she waited. Her patience and persistence paid off when the obscure blog from that teenager surfaced. "CrzyGrl204" gave just enough vague clues that, when coupled with the sightings from New Mexico, she was able to pinpoint a general area to search.

The people of Tolleson were generally friendly and open and loved to talk, making it easy, with carefully casual questions, to learn everything she needed to know. The house was called Gilfrey, and the woman named Katy.

The interloper.

She briefly felt sorry for the young woman, and that she would have to suffer so that Derrick could be taught a lesson. But her pity only lasted for a moment. If it weren't for that copper-haired girl and her seductive wiles, Charlotte wouldn't be forced to show the man she loved that he was *hers*, and there were consequences to his wandering eye.

Marriage, she scoffed. He actually believed that she would let him get *married*.

She stood and walked the short distance to the closet, opening the doors and kneeling into the enclosure, surrounding herself with his presence. The countless faces in countless still poses looked down on her, smiling and reassuring.

Breathing in deeply, she calmed herself. Not all was lost. She still had Katy's trust, despite the fact that the presence of the bodyguard had stopped her late night visits to the convenience store. Those had been fond hours; Katy had been incredibly sensitive, comforting her when Charlotte had rambled for hours about the neglect of the man she loved.

And not all was lost, despite the fact that the presence of the bodyguard had stopped the progression of the illness. He made it impossible to administer the poison unseen, and Katy had become progressively healthier.

Only a few more days, and everything would have been over.

But now, the wedding was in two days. Tomorrow, Derrick's family would arrive, and then later, he would. He would recognize her, and it would be too late.

She had to act now.

And then in a flash of blinding clarity, the answer came to her. It was so simple, she started to giggle. It was so easy. Why hadn't she thought of it before? Smiling, she stood and carefully closed the door of her closet—her haven—the resting place of the love of her life.

Soon, the madness would be over.

Chapter Twenty-One

A soft knock at the door pulled Katy from the letter she was writing, and she called out, "Come in!" as she signed her name to the bottom of the page. The door opened and Charlotte stuck her head in.

"Am I bothering you?" she asked, looking at the pages in Katy's lap. "I could come back another time."

"No, it's all right," she assured her, gesturing with her hand for her roommate to enter.

Jerry didn't trust her, but the woman was only misunderstood. Before the bodyguards showed up, Charlotte would come and visit Katy at night at the Slurp-N-Go, and she'd talk for hours about her husband and their relationship and how they used to be so close, and how he was never around anymore. She was lonely, and suffering from low self-esteem, and she was unsure of herself with his neglect. He never wrote her anymore, never called.

The more she relayed her story, the more Katy was glad that Caleb had asked her to stay with him and travel with him, and she only grew more and more confident in her decision to accept. She would not let time and distance come between them.

But she felt bad for her friend. Charlotte was suffering. And she'd been even more alone this last week, too shy to visit with the extra men around.

"I was thinking," the blonde began hesitantly. "I know that you have a lot on your mind and all, with the wedding only a few days away. But things have been a bit chaotic for you, and I thought maybe you'd like to take a breather and go swimming together, one last time."

"That's a great idea!" Katy said enthusiastically. "When would you like to go?"

"Well, if you weren't doing anything, I thought maybe we could go now," she shrugged. "I'm not sure if there will be another time."

Katy thought about it for a moment. The hour was late, it was after midnight. But her friend was right. If they didn't go now, they might not get another chance. She thought about waking Eddie, but it seemed silly. He was here to protect her from reporters, and so far there hadn't been any. And it was the middle of the night.

Nothing was going to happen.

"Give me a minute to change my clothes," she answered. "I'll meet you downstairs. We can sneak out together."

Charlotte smiled brilliantly before leaving the attic bedroom.

****

The bright moon sat high in the sky, illuminating the night and making the pathway bright. As they ambled along, Katy hummed to herself and skipped occasionally. She felt good. Her awful flu had finally gone away, the wedding plans were completed, and in a few hours, her future family would be arriving.

She was so excited, she could barely contain herself. She was going to have a sister and a mother and a father again. They'd talked on the phone several times to make arrangements, and they seemed incredibly nice. She could see that Caleb had gotten his sense of humor from his father, his impeccable manners from his mother, and his decency from both of them. Livy was so smart it was intimidating.

Charlotte sighed beside her. "What is Caleb

really like?" she asked.

"He's funny," she ruminated. "He's smart. You know, he could have gotten a full ride scholarship if he'd wanted it. By the time he got out of high school, he already had college credits because of the classes he was taking."

"So why did he give that up?" her companion questioned. "Why would he throw away his future like that?"

"He told me he chose to go into acting instead because it's what made him happy," she answered. "He figured college would always be there later, when he was ready. I think he's considering taking some classes now, though."

She could see Charlotte roll her eyes in the dim light, scoffing. "So he just walked away from his responsibilities so he could play?"

That made Katy pause, confused and irritated. "What are you talking about?" she asked gruffly. "What responsibilities was Caleb supposed to have at eighteen years old outside of planning for his future?"

"Oh… I don't know," was the vague answer.

They had reached the shore of the inlet where swimming was safe and, without saying another word, Charlotte peeled off her T-shirt and dove into the water. Katy was disgruntled, but followed the example. She dove into the water, letting cool velvet flow over her skin, caressing her, soothing away her discontent.

When she surfaced, her roommate was one foot away, staring at her intently with a hard look in her eyes that had never been there before. Her face was filled with malice, and for the first time, fear spiked through Katy's body.

She felt two legs wrap around her mid-section and lock into a vise grip. Before she could react, pressure dragged her downward and she barely had time to pull some air into her lungs before she was completely immersed. Just as quickly as she'd been dragged under, she was lifted again, gagging and flailing her arms in an attempt to get some stability. But those legs were still around her waist.

"He should have thought about the girlfriend he left behind!" Charlotte screamed.

The vice constricted again, twisting, and Katy was pushed under. She tried to pry the legs from her waist, but the hold was too strong and unrelenting. She reached out and pushed, pulled, grasped whatever she could grab hold of, all the while kicking her legs, desperate to get to the surface for some air. She felt silky, mottled fibers tangle in her fingers, and she pulled as hard as she could.

Fresh, relieving air broke over her face and she managed one giant gulp of oxygen before she submerged again. She could hear the splashing of their struggle underwater. She felt arms and legs surrounding her, fighting her, and she realized that she was losing. Her lungs began to burn, desperate. Her body tried to force her to open her mouth and inhale. Her strength waning, she knew that in another few seconds, the fight would be over.

She didn't think it possible, but the churning and tumultuous battle increased, her attacker squeezing harder, grasping at her more tightly for an instant. But they were being dragged and jostled and her face partially broke above surface. Her lungs took action of their own volition and pulled, sucking in a combination of water and air, causing her to choke and gasp, dragging more water and air into her body. Pinpricks of light danced in her vision and when all the pressure was suddenly gone, Katy was sure she was dying.

Arms encircled her from behind and she weakly tried to fight them off, knowing the battle was futile and already lost. She was moving in and out of consciousness.

"Be calm, I'm helping you!" a warm, familiar, feminine voice told her sternly through the haze before her vision turned black again.

She revived on the soft grass of the shoreline, choking and gagging up water as a fist pounded against her back. Her chest burned, but blessed air replaced the water, and she breathed in deeply several times, letting the oxygen revived her.

She felt her body shake all over, and the hand began to rub her back.

"Shhhh," Elizabeth soothed. "You're all right now."

Katy turned her head slightly to be greeted with sight of the older woman's relieved smile beaming down on her in the moonlight.

"You saved me," she gasped, her lungs on fire and her voice raspy.

"Don't try to talk," her rescuer said. "You're going to be all right." She paused hesitantly. "I need to go get some clothes on, before Sheriff Netter and Lonnie get here," she explained. "I'll be right over there."

At that moment, Katy realized that Elizabeth was completely naked, and she couldn't stop the wary expression from covering her face.

"I was skinny-dipping when I heard the fracas," the older woman explained, patting her on the shoulder. "It's usually peaceful and private at night. And I have my own secret place."

She winked and walked away out of sight, and Katy couldn't help but chuckle softly, painfully. She'd lived. But another alarming thought entered her mind, and she tried to sit up and look around as fear and panic began to swirl in her stomach.

"Charlotte?" she gasped worriedly.

"I don't know," Elizabeth said from several yards away. "She took off. I was more concerned with getting you to shore."

The sound of vehicles approaching announced the arrival of the sheriff and the EMTs. Katy felt silly as Lonnie and his partner took her vitals and tried to get her to lie down on a gurney in the back of the van while Netter interviewed Elizabeth. Katy adamantly refused to lie down, but finally compromised by sitting on one of the benches.

The trip to the small community hospital took half the time it should have, with the technician breaking every traffic law written, thrilled to have a police escort. He was disappointed that she wouldn't let him use his siren, insisting it lessened the whole experience and that she would regret it someday.

Somehow, she doubted it.

Within fifteen minutes, she found herself admitted to one of the few rooms, being attended to by two nurses and Doctor Ralph. They were bored, she was their only patient in several hours, and this was one of the most newsworthy things to happen in the area since the three-car pile-up back in December.

Katy just wanted to go home and go to sleep, but everyone kept insisting there was a legitimate medical reason for her to stay, and it wasn't to play rummy with Nurse Fairbanks. She wouldn't be able to leave for *at least* twenty four hours. If after that time there were no signs of pneumonia or other ill effects, they would let her go to her wedding.

All she could do was fume, because she had no clothes and it was too far to walk. No one would give her a ride. With no other option available to her, she did as she was instructed, and closed her eyes to rest, positive it wouldn't do any good.

It only felt like a few minutes later when Caleb stumbled into her hospital room looking worse then she felt. His wrinkled grey T-shirt sat lopsided over his chest. His short brownish-blondish-auburn-ish hair stood out in uneven clumps in a million directions. His eyes were bloodshot and the stubble on his chin reminded her of the first night they met. He even had the same weary, wild panicky look in his eyes.

"What are you doing here?" she asked groggily in way of greeting as he scooped her into his arms and proceeded to squash her. "I thought you had an interview tomorrow," she gasped in his hold.

"It was today," he mumbled into her hair. "It's been rescheduled."

"You shouldn't have done that," Katy reprimanded, trying unsuccessfully to pat him on the back, but the cords of some of the machines hooked up to her body limited her mobility.

"Katy, Katy, Katy," he sighed. "You cannot honestly believe that I'd stay away after what happened, do you?"

"Didn't anyone tell you I was fine?" she asked. "I wish they'd let me go home. Honestly. I'm fine. No permanent damage."

"I had to see for myself," he said, finally releasing her slightly to inspect for himself.

"No one will tell me anything," she grumbled petulantly. This wasn't like her, but she was feeling odd, and it seemed like someone else had taken over her emotions. One moment she was calm and serene, the next she wanted to scream, and in a moment, she might cry. But right now, she was peeved. "Have they caught Charlotte yet?"

"Don't worry," he said. "We're not going to let anything happen to you. Todd is—"

"So that's a no," she said, feeling the tears forming behind her eyes and, knowing that she wasn't going to be able to stop them, she felt helpless and angry again.

As the first drop escaped her eye, she hiccupped, and Caleb pulled her close into his arms again, guiding her head to his shoulders and rubbing her back like a little child.

"That's a no," he confirmed softly as she hitched. "They have roadblocks up, and her picture is circulating amongst every cop in the state, but they figure she's long gone by now." He paused for a second. I won't let anything happen to you, Katy. You are safe now, I promise."

She felt safe and protected in his arms, but she knew that it was her own fault that she'd been in danger in the first place. "Jerry was right," she sniffled. "I made it so easy for Charlotte. If Elizabeth hadn't been there..."

"But she *was* there," he reasoned. "She was a hero. I don't know why Eddie wasn't there," he added with a low, angry snarl. "But—"

"Don't be getting mad at Eddie, it wasn't his fault," she argued. "He did everything he could have done, short of sleeping in the stairwell in front of my door."

Caleb grunted, which could have meant anything.

Her eyes narrowed, her tears suddenly dry. "Caleb, you are not to do or say anything to make Eddie feel any worse about this than he already does."

"Or what?" he asked with a smirk.

"Or I will get very, very disappointed and upset."

She stared him in the eyes, unflinching as he pursed his lips and narrowed his eyes. "It was his job to protect you, and he failed at his job."

"Not through any effort of his own. Trust me. He was very annoying and overprotective for a full week and a half, and there was no sign of any danger anywhere. Charlotte was perfectly behaved that whole time, and I wasn't sick anymore. It was after midnight, everyone was in bed, and he was close enough that if I'd called out, he'd have been there in an instant. The man put a baby monitor in my room, for crying out loud. *I* turned it off. *I* snuck out of the house, despite the warnings. It was *my* fault."

Her fiancé let a heavy breath out through his nose and worked his jaw for a moment before his temper was under control. "Fine. Eddie won't get fired."

"Or chewed out."

"Or chewed out," he relented with a sigh. He paused. "You need your rest."

"I feel fine, they are being ridiculous. I haven't been able to sleep at all. How did you get here so fast, anyway?"

"Um… Katy, honey. It's about six in the morning. You were admitted five hours ago. I'd have been here sooner, but I couldn't get a flight."

"They drugged me!" she groaned and threw herself back against her pillows and tried to throw her arm across her eyes dramatically, but was hindered by the tubes and cords. "Ouch!"

"Careful!" Caleb admonished, helping to adjust all the paraphernalia.

"Your parents are going to be here in a few hours, and I'm stuck in here."

"Don't worry," he assured. "We're taking care of everything. The doctors have assured me that you are making great progress, and that they will most likely let you out in time to go to the wedding."

"Oh, wonderful", she said sarcastically, suddenly groggy again. "That's great reassurance."

"If they don't let you out, we'll either push it back a day, or do it here. Your choice. I don't care either way."

She yawned as she shot him a dirty look.

"But we'll cross that bridge if we come to it. No use borrowing trouble, right? You need to sleep."

"I can't," she said petulantly, yawning again.

Caleb chuckled. "I thought you might say that, so I brought some reading material."

He pushed himself away from her bed and rummaged through a duffel bag that had been dropped on the floor. Triumphant, he held up the object of his search and settled into the chair beside her pillow.

"What's on the venue now?" she asked, as they'd just finished reading the sequel to *The Alaria Chronicles*.

He smiled tenderly and settled back in his chair, opening his book with one hand to lie flat in his lap and grabbed her fingers with his free hand. "*Swiss Family Robinson*," he said. When she raised an eyebrow at his choice he squeezed her fingers gently. "I figured you already have enough scary thoughts right now."

She smiled, suddenly fighting tears again. She closed her eyes to hide them and his voice began to drift through the room, smooth and comforting. Everything was all right now. It was over. She was alive. Tomorrow, she would get married and live Happily Ever After.

Chapter Twenty-Two

Katy didn't want to sleep. Caleb was right; she had enough scary thoughts chasing through her mind right now and while she could keep them at bay while alert, her subconscious dredged them up the moment she quit focusing—and she couldn't focus on happy thoughts while asleep.

But the hospital staff sabotaged her, and so she dreamt. And when she dreamt, she was back in the water, looking into cold, malicious eyes while steel bands strangled her and pulled her under the surface. She struggled and fought while the splashing echoed around her all over again. The liquid burned her lungs, sending fire throughout her chest that snaked out to her limbs.

Her own gasping screams tore through the void, waking her to find that the binding cords were really Caleb's arms surrounding her, holding her, trying to comfort her. She struggled against his hold, pushing him away, feeling claustrophobic and desperately needing air. She wanted to breathe.

His arms dropped away, releasing her and he started to step away. But now he was too distant and she grasped his shirt in her fists before he could move farther. Yanking him closer, she wrapped her arms around his waist and sobbed uncontrollably onto his stomach.

"I'm not going anywhere," he whispered to her as he gently ran his fingers through her hair and rubbed her back. "I'm right here."

He was breathing deeply, calmly, and she began

to focus on the rhythm, letting the distraction soothe away the horror. Without trying, he grounded her, bringing her back to reality and washing away the terror. At last, her breathing matched his, her sobs finally under control.

"I don't want to sleep again," she stated firmly through a hiccup. "Don't let them do that again, please," she begged.

"You can't stay awake forever," he reasoned softly, apologetically.

"Not yet. Just give me some time."

He sighed. "Why don't you lie down again," he suggested. "It'll help if they don't think you're going to try to get up and run away the moment they aren't looking."

"I want to go home," she said again, for the millionth time, as she leaned back against the pillows.

"I know," he soothed. "Soon."

"You were right, you know," she told him regretfully. "I'm sorry."

"Don't you dare apologize for anything!" he commanded her with shock. "You—"

"You told me not to invite strangers any more. And I didn't listen. But you don't have to worry. It'll never happen again."

His whole face fell, and his sorrow somehow managed to compound tenfold. "Oh honey, don't talk like that. Don't let her strip you of yourself. Don't let her win."

"But you—"

"I bought the house on the other side of Gilfrey's, the one that's been empty for over a year," he interrupted her. "Ted and Jennifer are going to oversee it, and all you have to do is give a full name to Eddie for a background check. My security team is at your disposal. Use them."

"But—"

"Compromise," he told her. "It just took me too long to figure out what the compromise could be. If we'd done this earlier, maybe you would have been safe and—"

"This isn't your fault, Caleb!" she told him sternly, but the guilt in his eyes deepened. "I wouldn't have listened. I was so sure I was right and you were wrong. "

"Don't change who you are, Katy."

"I am changed." Her words made him wince, but she continued. "I'll find her again, eventually, the old Katy. But I need a little time."

He nodded. "I understand. I love you, no matter what."

He wouldn't meet her gaze as he sat down in the chair next to her holding her hand. She let him hide behind silence for a while, letting her nerves calm before confronting him.

"What aren't you telling me?" she finally asked.

He looked up with surprised irritation, but he merely scrunched his mouth to one side and gauged her mood before answering. "They caught her. Jerry had snapped a picture of Charlotte with her cell phone when she wasn't looking, and they circulated the picture throughout the entire state. They got her at the airport about thirty minutes ago."

Sharp relief washed through her, causing tears to threaten once more. Caleb dropped his eyes again, confusing her. This was good news, right?

"I know her," he sighed. "I know her well."

He should have thought about the girlfriend he left behind! Charlotte had screamed at her. "You were high school sweethearts," Katy said, and he nodded.

Sighing, he finally looked her in the eyes. "Her name is Trisha Nelson. To make a very long story short, she got pregnant a few months before graduation." He looked away to hide his emotions and squeezed her hand tightly before continuing.

"We argued about our future; she wanted me to give up acting and take the scholarship. I wanted the income to support her and the baby, and I hated school at that point. I already had enough in my savings from my previous movies to cover the cost of all her medical bills."

He paused then and, though he was trying hard to be unemotional and straightforward, he couldn't mask the pain that the memory brought him. "She went behind my back and got an abortion, thinking it would change my mind." He paused again, swallowing a few times before continuing. "I couldn't forgive her for killing my child, so I broke up with her. I haven't seen her since we graduated."

Katy didn't know what to do with that information. Her mind was blank, and all she could do was stare at the man sitting beside her sorrowfully. What a rotten story, He looked sad and scared.

"Do you hate me now?" he asked in trepidation.

"What?" she asked, incredulously. "How could I hate you? You were eighteen! And you obviously loved that baby."

He nodded. "I went to her first doctor's appointment with her. We got to hear the heartbeat and I was in love with it from that moment on."

She squeezed his fingers and he smiled at her gratefully, sadly, before clearing his throat.

"Trisha is a better actor than I am, Katy. We were in drama together all four years of high school, and she's a chameleon. She can become anyone."

"What's going to happen to her now?" Katy asked.

He shook his head and sighed. "She's been arrested. Any lawyer she gets will probably have her plead insanity, so she'll probably end up in an institution." He paused for a second. "I'm sorry that my past came back to hurt you like this. You have no idea how sorry I am that I've caused you pain."

"This isn't your fault," she told him and he scoffed. Gripping his hand tightly, she waited until he met her eyes. "It's not," she insisted.

And now it was her turn to comfort him. Sitting up, she draped her legs over the side of the bed and pulled him close, cradling his head to her stomach as his arms wrapped around her waist.

"I can't lose you," he mumbled.

"You won't," she assured, kissing his hair.

****

Finally declared healthy enough to be paroled, Katy was released from the hospital approximately two hours before the scheduled start of her wedding. Caleb had disappeared in the night sometime, and it was Elizabeth that pushed her obligatory wheelchair out to the car so that Jerry could drive her home.

The neighborhood was a circus of activity; she knew her neighbors were probably livid with their lawns and flowerbeds being trampled by the hundreds of reporters and cameramen. Police in their class A uniforms directed traffic, wrote citations and kept hundreds of vans and pedestrians off her private property.

Jerry pulled up alongside Officer Henderson and rolled down her window. "Hey Jayson," she greeted. "I see it hasn't let up at all."

The officer rolled his eyes and shook his head before standing up abruptly and waving to a woman running in their direction with a microphone, chased by a camera. "No interviews!" Henderson said. "If you come any closer, I will arrest you for trespassing!"

When the woman stopped her progress, he leaned back into the window. "It's good to see that you're all right, Katy. Everyone was really worried about you."

"I know," she told him. "Thank you. And if I don't get a chance to tell everyone before I leave tonight, can you thank the precinct for all the cards and flowers? They were lovely."

"No problem," he smiled and patted his hand on the door. "Better get going or you're going to be late for your own shindig! We'll keep the peace out here, don't worry about a thing." He smiled and winked at her, and his enthusiasm helped to normalize this absurd situation.

The next two hours were a blur of activity. She was rushed upstairs where Emily, Livy, Jerry and Elizabeth bathed, shampooed, pedicured, manicured, curled, braided, powdered, pampered and dressed. With barely enough time, everyone stood back and declared her perfect before whisking her downstairs to Ted.

He waited for her beside the kitchen door, casting nervous glances out the window to the crowd. "You ready, kid?" he asked as he turned to her. His eyes grew wide as he took in her daisy-covered braids and her elegant, simply cut white dress. Without a bead or sequin or any lace in sight, she almost looked as sophisticated as Jerry. If it hadn't been for the sunshine yellow heels, that is. "You look beautiful," he said with a smile. "Grandpa is proud right now."

It was the perfect thing to say, and she threw her arms around his shoulders, hugging him tightly. "I love you, Teddy!" she whispered. He was the only family she had left in the world. He was the one who was there when her world fell apart twice. He was her brother, and she would miss him this following year.

"I love you too, kid."

The sounds of Kyle's guitar floated into the kitchen and she saw Emily and Livy in their yellow dresses begin the march down the center of the chairs, headed toward the swing set where the minister waited under the garland-wreathed poles. The swings and chains had been temporarily removed and a wooden floor covered the wood chips, adding a makeshift gazebo feel to the occasion.

"That's our cue," Ted prompted and he held out his arm.

Breathing deeply, she took his offering and stepped through the door into the sunshine. All eyes turned to her, and she felt like she was a one-woman parade in front of the entire world. Rows upon rows of guests, and probably bodyguards, smiled at her as they turned in their seats, craning their necks to get a good look at the bride.

Countless children crowded in the tree house, watching as they leaned out the windows and door and railings. They even let Little Joey join them and he smiled and waved at her. She smiled and waved back, and some of her nervousness abated. These were her friends. They loved her.

And then she saw Caleb for the first time that day, and everyone else disappeared.

He stood at the end of the aisle in an old-fashioned tux, one that could have been considered at home in the nineteen thirties. It was midnight black, double breasted with wide lapels and a slightly cinched waist. His shirt was snowy white, made even starker by the blackness of his bow tie. On the lapel, he wore a yellow carnation. A sunshine yellow handkerchief peeked out the top of his pocket.

His hair was combed back, perfectly tamed for the very first time since she'd met him. He looked older somehow, more mature. They had both aged a few years over the last several days. It was amazing how your perspective changed, and how your priorities realigned themselves when you faced death. He smiled at her, his eyes echoing her own thoughts, and she knew that she was his entire world.

At last, she and her cousin finally reached him and Ted took her hand and placed it in Caleb's before stepping to the side.

He leaned over to her and whispered softly, "Your grandfather is here." He nodded slightly to indicate she should look behind them. Katy turned to see her favorite picture, the one she kept on her nightstand; the one Caleb had insisted he would hold at her graduation, perched on its very own chair, right in the front.

Without hesitation, without reserve, she threw her arms around her groom's neck and hugged him tightly. She could hear murmurs in the crowd behind them and a few chuckles, but she ignored them and kissed Caleb's cheek before turning to the minister again with a broad, watery smile.

Amused, the officiator pretended to look stern as he cleared his throat and opened his Bible. He began with a few words of advice, and she made a note to herself to ask him for a transcript later, because she was sure she wouldn't remember a single word. The vows were simple, but her entire heart was poured into them with rare solemnity. A few moments later Caleb looked into her eyes and told her that everything he had in the world, either physically, emotionally, or spiritually, was hers. He would cherish her forever.

The gold wedding bands they exchanged were simple, with no decoration or embellishment.

Finally, the minister declared them husband and wife, and told Caleb he could kiss his bride. With a wide tender smile, he pulled her into his arms and touched his lips to hers. The first kiss was brief, soft, and almost a sigh. But then he kissed her again, and the entire world dissolved around them.

She let herself get lost in the experience with the feel of her husband's arms around her, until the cheers finally intruded on their moment. Smiling at her, he leaned close to her ear and whispered, "We'll finish that later."

She blushed, smiling and turned to face their family and friends, feeling the happiest she'd ever felt in her entire life. Tomorrow would be challenging. Tomorrow, the world would intrude. But that would be tomorrow.

Today, right here, right now, she had her Happily Ever.

A word about the author...

Margie L. Miller lives with her husband, five boys, and a dog in central Arizona. She's wanted to be an author since the age of nine, when her third grade teacher made the mistake of telling her that her story "Detective Snoop and the Haunted House" was very good, instantly planting delusions of grandeur into her young, impressionable mind. Today, she keeps that first piece close, just to stay humble... and to get the occasional laugh. When not dragging her teenagers into various dubious adventures, she loves to read and crochet.

Thank you for purchasing
this Wild Rose Press publication.
For other wonderful stories of romance,
please visit our on-line bookstore at
www.thewildrosepress.com.

For questions or more information
contact us at
info@thewildrosepress.com.

The Wild Rose Press
www.TheWildRosePress.com

To visit with authors of The Wild Rose Press
join our yahoo loop at
http://groups.yahoo.com/group/thewildrosepress/

www.ingramcontent.com/pod-product-compliance
Lightning Source LLC
Chambersburg PA
CBHW061132200626
46817CB00016B/1231